BAILEIGH HIGGINS

Apocalypse Z - Book 1

Rise of the Undead

First edition

This book was professionally typeset on Reedsy.
Find out more at reedsy.com

Contents

Acknowledgments

Thank you to May Dawney for the lovely book cover design. You can check out her portfolio at https://covers.maydawney. com. She's a truly talented artist. A shout out to Graham Rintoul for his valuable input as well, and to all my friends and family for their support. I appreciate you all!

Dedication

I'd like to dedicate this book to Amy Donahue and Tara Lee. Thank you for all your support during my writing career. It's readers like you who make this a job worth doing!

Chapter 1 - Dylan

The people of Springfield thronged the entrance of the shopping center, jostling for space as they fought their way inside. Angry shouts were overlaid by shrill screams and the cries of frightened children. The blare of car alarms filled the parking lot, and columns of black smoke rose against the skyline. A single ambulance pushed its way through the dense traffic, the first one she'd seen all day despite the bloodshed.

Dylan grabbed a free shopping cart and added her struggles to the rest of the crowd, trying to get inside the supermarket. Coming here was a huge risk, but she needed food and water, or she'd never survive the coming days.

Gritting her teeth, she shoved her way through a gap between two middle-aged women. They screeched at her like banshees, their hostility palpable in the chaotic atmosphere, but she ignored them like the clucking chickens they were.

With her eyes set straight ahead, Dylan continued to forge a path through the mass of bodies blocking her way. She couldn't afford to care about anyone else or back down from a fight. It was every man for himself now, and people were desperate to survive. Desperate enough to kill, maim, or steal if need be. *And I don't plan on becoming a victim.*

She avoided the fridges and headed straight for the water,

cramming a case of plastic-wrapped bottles into the bottom of her cart. The canned aisle was next, and she focused her attention on protein and vegetables such as tuna, salmon, corn, peas, soups, and tomatoes. Among the dried goods, she found a few protein bars and packets of dried fruits and nuts.

It was a struggle. Every step of the way was a battle, and Dylan grew increasingly aware of the gun nestled against her hip and the crowbar clenched in her right hand. She hoped she wouldn't need either weapon, but that was becoming more unlikely with each passing second.

A toddler stared at her as she passed, its face swollen with tears while its young mother fought to get her hands on diapers and formula. Two men wrestled over a television, and she shook her head in wonder. What did any of that matter now? Three more were kicking another that lay prone on the floor, his head covered with his arms. Blood spattered their clothes, and they looked like savages.

Averting her gaze, Dylan ran through the last few aisles, grabbing anything useful she could get her hands on. Coffee, sugar, powdered milk, dried beans, rice, batteries, toilet paper, and vitamins.

Suddenly, a strange woman blocked her way, wielding a steak knife. Her eyes gleamed above nicotine-stained teeth, and her breath smelled of alcohol. "Give me your stuff. Now."

Dylan bared her teeth and growled. "Fuck off."

The woman waved the knife in front of her face. "I'm not telling you again, bitch. Give me your stuff."

"If you want it, take it," Dylan taunted.

The woman grabbed the cart with one hand and pulled, still waving her knife in the air. Gripping the crowbar with both hands, Dylan swung it at the woman's wrist. It connected with a loud crack, and the woman screamed as she dropped the knife from nerveless fingers. Letting go of the cart, she scrambled backward while holding her injured limb. "You bitch! You broke my arm!"

"You asked for it. Now scram!" Dylan said with a threatening wave of her weapon. The woman ducked away and disappeared into the press of bodies to look for easier prey, though Dylan doubted she'd be able to do much damage with her broken wrist. With a satisfied grin, she resumed her search for supplies.

As she reached the end of the aisle, the sounds inside the store changed in tone and pitch. Terrified screams rose all around her, a chant taken up by all as it passed around from mouth to mouth. Dylan froze to the spot as she fought to make out the words. When she did, all the blood drained from her face, leaving her cold and numb.

"The dead!"

"They're coming!"

"Get inside!"

"Block the entrance!"

People stampeded away from the doors. They pushed their way deeper into the store to get away from the horror that approached from the outside. Dylan knew only too well what it was, and fear spurted through her veins at the thought.

Desperation fueled her actions, and she pulled back from the surging mass of bodies before she could be crushed or trampled underfoot. Using her shopping cart as a battering ram, Dylan forged a path to the back of the store where a familiar door awaited.

Staff Only.

It led toward the storage room and loading bay at the back of the store, as well as the manager's office, staff quarters, and

3

bathrooms. She'd spent a few months during the last year working at the supermarket as a bagger. It was the reason she chose this place above all the others that were closer to home. The reason she carried her old keycard in her pocket, praying she wouldn't need it, but hoping it would still work if she did.

Dylan reached her destination and pulled up to the heavy iron door, usually locked to prevent easy access. With fumbling fingers, she pulled out her card and ran it through the slot. A negative beep sounded, and the red light shined. "No!"

Behind her, the screams were growing louder, and she frantically tried again, but to no avail. The store had become a deathtrap. The crush of panicking people grew worse, and she was pushed up against the door with her loaded cart pressed painfully into her midriff.

Gasping for breath, Dylan scanned the walls and ceiling for an escape. Any escape. Abandoning her supplies was better than dying for them. A few windows set high in the walls beckoned, as did the fire escape on the far side. Could she make it to any of them?

A shoulder rammed into her side, and Dylan hissed as her ribs exploded in red-hot agony. She almost lost her grip on the cart, but managed to hold on as she fell to the floor.

She looked up in time to see the nearest rack topple over with a ponderous groan. It crashed on top of her, and only the shopping cart prevented her from being crushed. Bottles of bleach and disinfectant burst on impact, and harsh fumes burned her nostrils.

Through tear-filled eyes, she gazed around in horror. Many had not been as lucky as her, and several people were trapped or injured. The rest of the store continued its rampage of terror, the crowd killing itself as it tried to escape the dead.

Even as she stared, jerky figures entered the store and sprinted toward the nearest victims. With guttural growls, they pounced on their prey, digging their teeth and nails into any open flesh they could reach. The coppery scent of blood filled the air, and the masses were whipped into a frenzy as death approached.

Pinned between the wall and her cart, Dylan was trapped. No amount of wriggling or pushing could get the rack to shift even an inch. Sitting in a puddle of bleach, she closed her eyes and tried to regain a semblance of calm. "There has to be a way out. There has to."

A low snarl caused her eyes to pop open, and she found herself looking at one of the infected. He was perched on top of the debris like a hungry wolf, his teeth bared in a threatening grimace. Black veins crisscrossed his pale skin. There was something primal about him, something so wild she knew there could be no reasoning with such a creature. He was no longer human.

With her heart pounding in her chest, she watched him sniff at the crushed bottles of cleaning supplies, wrinkling his nose at the sharp smell. An injured woman groaned, and he honed in on her with deadly intensity. Pouncing like a tiger, he tore into the helpless woman's throat, and her screams were lost in a gurgling fountain of blood.

Dylan pressed her hands to her lips to contain her screams, but the horror was too overwhelming. Not caring who or what heard her, she twisted around and slammed her fists against the door behind her. "Somebody help me! Please!"

Undiluted fear coursed through her veins like acid, and she kept yelling and banging until her throat grew raw. A snarl caused her to look back. The infected man prowled toward her on all fours, blood dripping from his chin.

Dylan twisted to the side, reaching for her gun. Her hand closed on the pistol grip, and she pulled it free from its holster. Breathing hard, she sought to still her trembling hands. *Remember your training. You didn't spend all those afternoons at the range for nothing.*

The infected paused, and his thigh muscles bunched, ready to leap. She took careful aim. He was so close. Too close. *It has to be the head. That's what the CDC said in their last broadcast.*

As she pulled the trigger, a silly thought occurred to her. *Why was it always the damn head?*

The bullet drilled a hole between the man's eyes, and he collapsed with half of his skull missing. The next moment, Dylan fell backward as the door behind her opened without warning. A set of familiar blue eyes gazed down into hers, and she gasped with surprise. "Ben? Ben Randall?"

"Dylan? Is that you?" he asked.

She nodded, pathetically grateful to see her old manager. He'd always been good to her, and she prayed he still liked her enough to help her. "It's me."

He grabbed her by the arms and hauled her to her feet. "Hurry. They're coming!"

Dylan glanced at the inside of the supermarket and blanched. Every infected inside the space was running toward them, drawn by the gunshot. Her eyes fell on her cart, and her lips compressed. "I'm not leaving my stuff."

Jamming the gun back into its holster, she grabbed the cart's handles and yanked it toward her. It rolled inside, and she slammed the door shut with a yell of defiance. An avalanche of crap had followed the cart, however, and the door caught on a bottle of laundry detergent. "Oh, shit."

6

Kicking at the bottle with her foot, Dylan tried to clear the way, but it was hooked on something and refused to budge. An infected woman reached the entrance and threw herself at it with a screech. Her hand thrust through the opening and reached for Dylan's face. She ripped out a clump of hair, and tears filled Dylan's eyes. More infected followed, howling like wolves.

Desperate to shut the door, Dylan grabbed the woman by the wrist and pushed. "Get out!"

The infected woman was as slippery as an eel, but Dylan refused to give up. Sharp pain lanced up her forearm as the woman attacked her exposed flesh, but she couldn't let go.

At the same time, Ben yanked the blockage away from the door and yelled. "Close it now!"

Dylan slammed it shut and the lock clicked into place, sealing them inside the storage room. Silence fell, broken only by their harsh breathing. The infected beat on the door, but the steel was thick, and it only registered as dull thuds. They were safe. For the moment.

On wobbly legs, Dylan stumbled toward the nearest crate. She wiped the sweat and tears from her face. Everything smelled like bleach, and her clothes were soaked with the stuff. Her scalp burned where she was missing a hank of hair, and her limbs were stiff and bruised.

Despite this, Dylan managed a tremulous smile as she looked at her rescuer. "We made it. Now, we just have to get out of here."

Ben stared at her with a grim expression, his spectacles slightly askew on his face. Somehow, that detail bothered her more than anything else. She'd never seen him with so much as a hair out of place. He was always painfully neat and tidy.

"I'm sorry, Dylan, but you're on your own."

The fluorescent light above their heads flickered, casting Ben's face into shadow for a second. She frowned, unable to comprehend his words. "What do you mean? Surely, it makes sense to stick together. At least until we get out of here."

As he shook his head, he pointed at her arms resting on her knees. "That zombie bit you, Dylan. You're not going anywhere."

She stared at him for a breathless moment before dropping her gaze. Her eyes fixed on the tender flesh of her forearm, the skin smooth and unbroken except for a few scratches caused by long fingernails...and a half-moon crescent that leaked tiny droplets of blood. She sucked in a deep breath. When had that happened? She'd never even noticed it during the struggle.

It was a small wound. Not deep enough to warrant a single stitch, but it was more than enough to kill her. To send the virus tumbling through her bloodstream and into her brain. The world around her faded away as Dylan faced the undeniable truth. "I'm infected."

Chapter 2 - Amy

Amy stared at the freshly dug grave at her feet. It was shallow. Barely three feet deep. The earth formed a mound at her side, and its rich scent lingered in her nostrils. It mingled with the smell of decay, a cloying sweetness that stuck to the roof of her mouth.

A single tear ran down her face. It was all she had left. She was all cried out after the events of the past few days.

They saw it on the news. The reports were hard to believe at first. Fantastical. Who in their right minds believed in a zombie apocalypse? Especially in Louisville, Kentucky, with its lush green countryside and friendly people. It was absurd. But, the video footage was impossible to ignore, and when a National Emergency was announced, they had no choice but to take the crazy stories seriously.

Her dad left first, driving off in his beat-up old truck to buy supplies. He never came back. Next, it was her mom. She took off in the early morning hours while Amy was still asleep. She returned hours later with a trunk full of food and toiletries. That wasn't all she brought home, however.

Amy shook her head. The memory of her last conversation with her mom surfaced again. It kept doing that. No matter how hard she tried, it insisted on coming back, over and over again.

***

"Listen to me, sweetheart. You have to do what I say," Amy's mom said, steering her away from the main bedroom. "Your father's gone."

"No, that's not true. It can't be," Amy cried, unwilling to believe that her father, the strongest man she knew, was dead. Or even worse. A zombie.

Amy's mom shook her by the shoulders. "You have to accept the facts, Amy. He's not coming back. If he could've, he would've been here."

"No," Amy said, fighting against the knowledge that welled up inside. Her mother was right, she knew it, but she wasn't ready to accept it. Not yet.

"Come now." Amy's mom tugged on her arm again, pulling her toward the stairs. "You have to focus."

"Why?" Amy asked though she knew the answer to the question already. It was written in her mom's waxen skin, the sweat that beaded on her forehead, the blood that stained the bandage on her arm. She was infected, doomed to become a zombie — a flesh-seeking cannibal.

"Because very soon, you'll be on your own. At least until your brother gets here," Amy's mom replied. "He's on his way. He said so, but until then, you have to look after yourself."

"Mom, please," Amy begged, yanking her arm back. "I can't do this alone. I need you."

"Yes, you can. You're sixteen, not a child anymore." Her mom paused, staring at her with sad eyes. "I can't protect you any longer. It's up to you now. This is the moment when you decide whether you want to live or die. I can't make that decision for you."

"But how? What do I do?" Amy asked, clinging to her mother's hand, aware how clammy her skin felt. How hot.

"Stay here until Alex arrives. It'll be a few days at most. There is enough food and water to last you a couple of weeks, and there's fuel in the generator if the power goes off."

"I don't want to wait here all alone," Amy protested. "What if those things come here?"

"You'll be safe. The farm is isolated, and the fence will keep them out. All you need to do is be careful."

"What about you?" Amy asked, tears burning her eyelids.

"Very soon, I'll turn into one of those things. A monster. I can't let that happen." Amy's mom gripped her elbow and led her downstairs to the living room. She pushed Amy into a chair. "Wait here."

Amy perched on the edge of the seat, tugging at the worn material of her jeans with nervous fingers. She gazed around the room. This was her home. What would it be like without her parents? She couldn't imagine it. "This isn't happening. It can't be. Dad will come home, and Mom...she'll be fine. It's just a small bite mark."

But Amy knew she was kidding herself, telling a lie that even she couldn't believe. Not after everything she'd seen on tv. The internet. In town.

Her mother returned from the basement with a shotgun, a Glock 43, and a box full of ammunition. She handed the shotgun and ammo to Amy. "I took this out of the safe. You'll need it. Don't go anywhere without it, okay?"

Amy nodded, unable to reply. The gun was heavy, the steel barrel cold to the touch, but she was used to it. Her father had taught her to shoot from a young age, and she'd spent many a day out in the woods hunting birds and small game. She was proficient with both the 12 gauge pump-action shotgun and her dad's .303, but he'd taken that with him when he left.

On autopilot, she checked that the gun was fully loaded with the safety on. As per regulation, it only took three shells, so it would be better to carry a pistol as well for backup. The action soothed her anxiety somewhat and reminded her that she could defend herself. She wasn't just some wallflower in need of rescuing. She glanced at her mother who bustled around with nervous energy. "So, what now?"

"Lie low, keep the windows and doors shut, and wait for Alex. Last we spoke, he was only two or three days out depending on the road conditions. He'll know what to do when he gets here."

"Alright."

"There's a first-aid kit in the linen cupboard if you need it," her mom said, fiddling with the porcelain figurines on the mantelpiece. "And the keys to my car are on the board in the kitchen next to the safe keys. There's cash in the safe too. It might not help much, but who knows."

"Okay." The word sounded dull and lifeless, much like Amy did herself.

Her mom stopped fidgeting and turned to face her. "Oh, my child. I'm so sorry this is happening to you. I wish I could take it all away, but I can't. You have to be strong now. You and Alex…you have to live. For your dad and me. For us."

Amy swallowed on the knot that had formed in her throat, her voice thick when she spoke. "I'll try."

"Promise?"

"I promise."

"Come here, sweetheart. We need to say goodbye."

Amy jumped up and ran into her mother's waiting arms,

the embrace bittersweet. The wall that was holding back her tears burst, and she sobbed in earnest, not caring that she was messing all over her mom's dress. "I'm gonna miss you, Mom. So much."

"I know, sweetheart, but I'll always be with you. Always," her mother whispered.

"I love you," Amy said.

"I love you too. Forever and always."

After a long time, they pulled apart, and Amy watched her mom walk upstairs, pistol in hand. When the shot rang out, her knees gave in. She collapsed to the floor, and curled into a ball, mourning her loss with wracking sobs that threatened to rip her apart. This was it. The moment when everything changed.

***

Amy shook her head to clear the memory. She had to concentrate. There was still so much to do. With a grunt of effort, she dragged her mother's body into the shallow grave she'd dug.

The corpse was wrapped in linen. She didn't want to look at her mother's dead face again, her skull deformed by the pistol shot. It had been bad enough cleaning the mess in her parent's bathroom, and she didn't think she'd ever be able to set foot inside it again. No. She wanted to remember her mom as she used to be. Warm, loving, and beautiful. A shining light who welcomed all into her heart and home with open arms.

Taking up the shovel, Amy closed the grave one spadeful of earth at a time. She winced when the fresh blisters on her palms burst but kept at it. Her blood dripped onto the ground. An offering. A final farewell. "Goodbye, Mom. I'll always love you. Say hi to dad for me."

After saying a prayer, Amy walked to the house with the shotgun slung across her back. The sun was setting, its golden rays fading to mauve on the horizon. Night was falling, and with it would come the darkness. "I'd better be ready for it."

Chapter 3 - Alex

For the umpteenth time, Alex tried to call his mother. Nothing. It went straight to voicemail. Ever since the shit hit the fan, reception had been spotty. He glanced up and down the street, aware that his uniform was attracting attention. That was the last thing he wanted, especially at a time like this.

When he first heard about the outbreak, he thought it was a joke. So did his army buddies. But when they were dispatched to deal with a particularly violent riot, he got to see firsthand what they were up against. It wasn't pretty.

Even now, the memory was enough to give him nightmares. He'd seen things that couldn't be explained. Horrifying things: A mother attacking her own children. A man getting back to his feet after a fellow soldier emptied half a magazine into his chest. People eating people.

It didn't take long to figure out they weren't human anymore. They felt no pain, didn't get tired, didn't sleep, and couldn't be reasoned with. They were dead. Only now, death was no longer the end. It was just the beginning.

At first, he did his duty and followed orders. He believed, as they all did, that the outbreak could be stopped and the zombie menace eradicated. He was wrong. Within days, millions were infected. Key installations fell to the undead hordes, major cities burned, and the infrastructure began a slow collapse beneath the strain. It wasn't long before he made up his mind to leave. His family needed him. He wasn't the only one, either. A bunch of other soldiers had the same idea. It was every man for himself now.

That didn't mean he wouldn't get into trouble if caught, however. The army was still very much the army. A stickler for the rules and they did not tolerate deserters.

Alex ignored the curious glances of onlookers and ducked into an alleyway. After making sure it was empty, he pressed dial on his phone again. "Come on, Mom. Answer."

The phone rang and after a few seconds, connected. "Alex? Is that you?"

"Mom! Yes, it's me." Relief flooded his veins.

"Oh, thank goodness. I was so worried. Are you okay?" she asked.

"I'm fine."

"Are you sure? I've been watching the news, and it's just terrible. All those units falling. I was scared you were one of them."

"No, Mom. I'm still here, alive. Promise."

"Where are you?" she asked.

"In Kansas City, Missouri. I left the army," he replied.

"Why?" she asked with a gasp.

"Because, I'm coming home, Mom. You guys need me. After what I've seen, this is not going to blow over," he explained.

"Are you sure? Won't you get into trouble?" she asked.

"Not if I'm careful," he replied. "What about you guys? Are you okay?"

"Oh, sweetie. I don't know how to say this, but your dad…your dad's gone."

16

"Gone? What do you mean gone?" he asked, a sense of dread settling on his shoulders.

"He went to town for supplies and never returned. But that's not all, sweetie. I...I went myself this morning to look for him, and I was attacked."

Alex's blood ran cold. "Don't say it, Mom. Please, don't."

"I was infected, Alex. That man bit me," she said, confirming his worst fears.

A long silence ensued as neither knew what more to say. A knot formed in Alex's throat, and he swallowed hard to contain his grief. "What...what about Amy?"

"Amy's fine for now, but she needs you. When can you get here?"

"It's a seven hour drive from here to Louisville, give or take, but with the road conditions, I'd say a day or two. Maybe three."

"Well, she should be okay until then. She's got food, water, and the shotgun."

"What about you?" he asked, though he didn't really want to know the answer.

"Don't worry about me, sweetheart. I'll take care of it. Just make sure you get here. Amy needs you. She's too young to survive on her own."

"I know. I'm on my way."

"Promise me, Alex," she said, her voice hardening. "I need to know you'll keep your promise, no matter what."

"I swear it, Mom. I'll protect Amy. No matter what."

His mother sighed, her voice breaking on her next words. "I love you, sweetheart. Never forget that."

"I love you too, Mom."

She hung up, and for a long time, Alex stared at the phone in his hands. Grief and loss weighed heavy on his heart, turning it into a block of ice. In the span of one single phone call, he'd lost nearly his entire family. He knew what his mom was planning. He'd heard it in her voice.

After a while, Alex straightened his shoulders and shouldered his rucksack, conscious that time was running out. He needed to get back home before something happened to Amy.

He stepped out of the alley and merged with the crowd of people flocking the street. They were all of one mind. To gather as many supplies as they could. At least, most of them. Some were more interested in looting riches and settling petty scores. That much was evident by the sound of screaming and breaking glass.

It amazed him that so many seemed unaware of the seriousness of the situation. Evidence of the outbreak was everywhere, though it had yet to hit them full force. Police vans rushed past with their wailing sirens. Ambulances tried to cope with the growing number of casualties and failed. Numerous car crashes blocked narrow roads, and the traffic was hell.

Alex quickened his step but paused when he spotted a clothing shop. He ducked inside and grabbed a few things. The harassed cashier rang up the items and accepted the handful of crumpled dollar bills Alex threw at him. He'd taken the time earlier to withdraw all his savings and carried a thick wad of cash around. He took care to hide it, aware that even now people would kill for so much money.

"What are you still doing here?" he asked the cashier.

The guy shrugged. "I need the job."

"You know there are zombies out there, right?"

"That's what I've got this for," the cashier said, pulling a revolver out of the back of his pants.

Alex tried and failed to look impressed. He'd seen up close what the zombies could do, and one gun wouldn't cut it. People needed to band together and hole up in fortified positions if they were to stand any chance at all. Not that the cashier would believe him, that much was clear from the guy's attitude.

"Can I use your change room?" he asked instead.

"Sure, man. Whatever," the cashier replied.

Alex rushed into the nearest cubicle and stripped off his uniform. Much as it had served him in the past, now it was a liability. He pulled on the jeans, t-shirt, and jacket he'd chosen, but kept his army belt and boots. They were too useful to ditch. Onto the belt, he hung his standard issue Beretta M9 in its holster plus a sheath carrying his combat knife. After folding up his uniform, he tucked it into his rucksack next to his other belongings and hoisted it onto his shoulder.

This time, he blended right into the crowd when he stepped onto the curb. To them, he was just another civilian out to grab what he could. Alex had a different goal in mind, though. He needed transport, and he needed it in a hurry.

Kansas City was still holding it together, but barely. Vehicles from the National Guard drove around, announcing that a safe zone had been set up just outside the city limits. They were encouraging people to go there, and Alex supposed it was the best option for most civilians unable to defend themselves. It wasn't for him, however.

After jogging three blocks, the sign of a second-hand motor-cycle dealership caught his eye. "Exactly what I need."

He angled across the street, jumping to the side to avoid getting hit by a sedan. It raced past, and he caught sight of the frightened faces of a couple of kids in the backseat. In the distance, he heard the muffled pops of gunshots followed by wild screams. It had to be an outbreak. The city was going to the dogs, and he had better hurry.

Alex entered the dealership seconds later and was surprised to find the owner dawdling behind his desk. The poor guy didn't appear to have a clue, even when Alex warned him worse was to come. "You should go home to your family. It's getting crazy out there."

"And miss out on a sale?" the guy scoffed. "This will all blow over soon, mark my words. They've dispatched the army, for crying out loud."

Alex shook his head in disbelief, but he didn't have time to argue. Not unless he wanted to be trapped inside the exposed shop with its three glass walls and a lone idiot for company. Instead, he rushed around the showroom and inspected the bikes on offer. Quickly, he made his choice.

"I want that one," he said, pointing at a Suzuki V-Strom 1000 ABS. The bike had two saddlebags attached to the sides for storage, and the previous owner had equipped it with dirt tires. It was perfect for both on and off-road use, which was exactly what Alex wanted. He couldn't afford to get stuck in the bumper to bumper traffic.

After a minute of fierce haggling, Alex paid with the last of his cash. The deal included a full tank of fuel plus two jerry cans extra which he tied onto the back seat. He also got to pick out a helmet, gloves, and a leather jacket for protection.

He transferred his belongings to the panniers: A canteen of water, a basic first-aid kit, a couple of MRE's, extra ammunition, a toothbrush, and fresh socks and underwear. He had to ditch his uniform, however. No space. His M4A1 carbine went onto his back with the sling across his chest.

Satisfied, he climbed onto the bike and started the engine. It roared to life, and he revved it with an experimental twist of the wrist. "She's got power, alright. Just what I need."

He shot the owner a quick salute, ready to take off. "Thanks."

"What about the paperwork and registration?" the owner cried, wringing his hands together.

"I'll be back for it," Alex said, the lie sliding off his tongue like silk.

"You can't do that!"

"Watch me."

Before the owner could stop him, Alex pointed the bike at the exit and zipped out of the building onto the street. The bike was fast and responsive. As he weaved through the traffic with smooth precision, Alex found himself grinning with pure pleasure. Nothing could stop him now. He'd be back home in no time at all. "Hold on, Amy. I'm coming, Sis."

Chapter 4 - Dylan

"What do I do now, Ben?" Dylan asked in a low whisper. She shifted around on the rough crate she sat on, trying to get comfortable. It was impossible. The crate wasn't meant for sitting or comfort. Not that it mattered in the face of what had befallen her. She was going to die anyway.

Ben shook his head, unable to comfort her. "I don't know."

A single tear leaked from the corner of her eye, but other than that she felt numb. "I knew I shouldn't have come. I should've stayed at home."

"I'm sorry." He got up and paced around the room, avoiding the stacked pallets of supplies around them. The dull thuds of the infected beating on the door had grown distant, like something from another world.

"To think I got bitten because of that stupid cart," Dylan said, giving the offending object an angry kick. "I should've let it go. Instead, I came all this way to die for a few bottles of water and a couple of cans of tuna. I don't even like tuna!"

"It's crazy," Ben agreed, his shoulders sagging with defeat. "I wish there was something I could do."

"I know." Dylan glanced back at the way she came. "At least, you saved me from being eaten and becoming one of those things straight away. Now, I can go out on my own terms."

Ben glanced at the gun on her hip. "I suppose it's better to go by your own hand than..."

He trailed off, and Dylan shuddered. She knew what he meant. They both knew what awaited her, and it wasn't pretty. Her thoughts wandered back over the past few weeks and how it all began.

It started as an internet rumor, circulating on the web via a series of posts, videos, and chatroom threads. There was a health alert in the Congo, North Africa. Something about an outbreak in Brazzaville. Like many, she didn't believe it, writing it off as fake news. Then it aired on the news, hitting all the big channels in a row. By then, it was too late.

Within days, half of the world's population were sick. Once infected, patients grew increasingly ill with flu-like symptoms. They continued to work and travel, spreading the infection until forced to seek medical care.

The hospitals and medical centers overflowed as doctors sought to treat them. None survived. Within seventy-two hours, the virus ran its course, killing the host only to reanimate the corpse minutes later.

Those that didn't succumb initially were killed by those that did — ripped apart by the monsters that used to be their family, friends, and colleagues. While some were immune to the airborne strain, no one was immune to a bite. Minutes later they rose from the dead, turned into monsters as well. If bitten but not killed outright, like Dylan, you had time. Seventy-two hours, give or take.

Time to suffer the full horror of the infection as it ravaged your body.

Time to feel the virus take over your brain and wash away everything that made you human.

Time to regret all the things you never got to experience.

Dylan looked at the bite mark on her arm, tracing its shape with her forefinger. "I've got no one to say goodbye to."

"Excuse me?" Ben said with a frown.

"Never mind. Just thinking out loud." Dylan twisted her arm around and set her digital watch to stopwatch mode. Thumbing in the hours minus ten minutes for time already passed, she watched as the seconds began to run backward. Seventy-one hours, forty-nine minutes, and fifty-two seconds.

"Do you have someone?" Ben asked after an uncomfortable silence. "Someone to look after you when the…you know. When the time comes."

Dylan snorted. "Nothing's changed in that regard, Ben. It's still just me."

He sighed. "I'm sorry, but I have to get back to my family. Are you going to be alright?"

Dylan stared at him with raised eyebrows, the irony of his question not lost on her. "I'll be fine, thanks."

He bobbed his head without meeting her gaze and walked toward the door that opened onto the loading dock at the back of the supermarket. After gazing outside through a side window, he said, "The coast is clear for now. You can make a run for it if you want, or you can stay here. Your choice."

"I'm going," Dylan said. "I'll be damned if I stay here."

"Where's your car parked?" he asked.

"Out front."

"You'll never make it."

"I know. Can you give me a lift?" Dylan asked, knowing he always parked at the back with the other employees.

"I can't, Dylan. I've been gone too long already. I'm sorry, but my family needs me, and I can't take you with me. It's too risky."

"Then why didn't you stay at home with them?" Dylan said with growing frustration.

"Same reason you did. Food. I loaded my car with the supplies in here while…"

"While the people out front were dying," Dylan said, not bothering to hide her bitterness.

"Try to understand. I've got kids, a wife, a dog, for God's sake," Ben said, running a nervous hand through his thinning hair. "They're my responsibility."

Dylan sighed, knowing he was right. "I get it, Ben. I do."

"Look, Susan came in as well. Her car's parked next to mine, and her keys are in her locker."

"Where's Susan?"

Ben didn't reply, and Dylan got the message. Susan was dead.

"I'm going now," he said, "before those things can circle around. You should too."

"I'm coming, just give me a chance to grab a few things," Dylan said.

"I can't wait any longer." After a final look outside, he slid his keycard through the slot and opened the door a crack. When nothing happened, he tossed her the card. "Take this, and God be with you, Dylan."

With those final words, he ducked outside. The door swung shut behind him and automatically locked itself, sealing her in.

Dylan stared at space he'd occupied moments earlier and fought back the despair that threatened to weigh her down. Ben. The first friendly face she'd seen since this whole nightmare began. Gone. Just gone.

"Alone again," she whispered. "Always alone."

Chapter 5 - Dylan

Dylan took a few seconds to collect herself. She had to face the facts. She was infected. Within three days, after suffering through the various symptoms presented by the virus, she'd die and turn into a flesh-eating monster unless she ended things herself.

"Well," Dylan huffed, wiping away her tears. "I'm certainly not dying in this shithole."

With fresh determination, she walked toward the staff room next to the supply room. The manager's office, Ben's old office, abutted it. They were the only other rooms in the building besides the toilets.

Susan's locker was open, her car keys and handbag discarded inside. Dylan took the keys and ran back to the exit. A quick look through the windows showed her it was all clear for the moment, and she located Susan's sedan with ease. It was parked nearby, and after a moment's hesitation, she slipped outside.

With her heart banging in her throat, Dylan opened the driver's door and left it ajar. Then she opened the trunk before running back inside the shopping center. "I'll be damned if I starve to death before I die."

Grabbing the cart that had doomed her, she pushed it to the car and loaded the contents into the trunk with supersonic speed. The hair on the back of her neck prickled. The longer she was exposed and out in the open, the more scared she got. Once it was done, she slammed the lid shut and jumped behind the wheel. "Time to get out of here."

The car was ancient, but Susan had looked after the old thing, and the engine started without a hitch. She edged out of the parking, her head swiveling as she searched for zombies, but they hadn't found the back of the store yet.

Not wasting a moment further, Dylan gunned it, racing out of the parking lot with a squeal of burning rubber. In the rearview mirror, she watched the undead pour out of the store's entrance like cockroaches. They trampled each other in their haste to chase her down, their jerky movements at odds with their speed.

"The fuckers just had to be fast, didn't they?" Dylan muttered while rummaging in her pockets for a cigarette. "Like the end of the world isn't bad enough already."

Dylan left the lot behind and headed deeper into town. She lit a smoke and dragged on it until her lungs burned, still unable to wrap her head around her imminent death. She glanced at the bite mark on her arm and shook her head. "Unbelievable."

There was an icy chill in the air, and she cranked up the heat, grateful for the warm air that blasted through the vents. It was still early, around ten in the morning, but the gray clouds promised little sun. Winter was here to stay, its presence made clear by the skeletal branches on the trees and the cold wind that cut to the bone.

At first, Dylan drove blindly, not caring where she went. The golf course streamed past, followed by Starbucks and McDonalds. A couple of teens ran across the street, not sparing her a glance, and she wondered where they were going. It was dangerous out on the streets, and they were likely up to no good.

A mob clamored at the doors of a gunshop, screaming to get in. The owner had locked up tight, however, the reinforced doors repelling any looters. She knew the place. A few days earlier, she'd been lucky to get in and buy the Glock 17 she now carried on her hip, complete with a holster and seventeen round magazine.

The owner had been kind, probably because she'd spent so many hours on his gun range practicing. It'd had been mostly for fun, a hobby she enjoyed, at first. Now she was glad she'd done it and was a fair shot with most weapons. She only had twelve bullets left, though, which placed her at a decided disadvantage.

"Ah, well. I'll just have to make do until I can get more," she muttered.

With a tight grip on the steering wheel, she navigated the clogged streets. It was a mess of abandoned cars, wrecks, and groups of undead that wandered about looking for a meal. Any living people stayed well out of sight, hiding behind boarded-up windows and locked doors.

She'd already decided not to go home. Nothing waited for her there. Nothing but rusted water pipes, possibly undead neighbors, and peeling wallpaper. "Face it, Dylan. You live in a dump. I guess some things never change."

Her mind wandered back to her childhood. The little that she'd had of it anyway. Abandoned on the church steps as a baby, she'd never known her parents, never had the luxury of a real home. Passed from one foster home to the next, she ended up in juvie when the latest foster dad got too friendly, drawn by her dark red hair, blue-green eyes, and budding curves. It earned him nothing but a stab wound to the gut. The asshole survived and made sure she was blamed for the incident.

At eighteen, she aged out of the system and was tossed into society with little to her name but the will to survive. Six years later, she still hadn't made her mark or achieved anything of note, traveling from one place to the next as the fancy took her. *At least, I never became a junkie or a prostitute.*

Now Dylan had no idea what to do or where to go. She rolled to a stop at a crossing and stared in every direction. Behind her lay Springfield, Illinois, the town she'd called home for the past year, though it had never truly felt that way. Not that any place felt like home. She was just passing through. A tourist. An outsider.

To the South-West lay St. Louis, a death trap, for sure, and to the South-East was Edinburg, Sharpsburg and a whole host of other small towns much like the next. Undecided, she blew out a frustrated breath. "Why is this so hard?"

Dylan banged her head against the headrest of her seat until she remembered something. Or rather, someone. A familiar face from the past. "Frankie."

Frankie, short for Francine, was probably the closest thing she'd ever had to a friend. During a brief stint in Sharpsburg, they'd worked together at a diner and even shared an apartment for a few weeks. Though total opposites, they somehow clicked and hit it off. Many of Dylan's best memories stemmed from their brief friendship, but, after a few months, she'd grown restless. Driven by some inexplicable need, she'd moved on to the bigger and brighter city lights of Springfield while Frankie stayed behind. Time passed, and the two spoke less and less until the conversation dried up completely. Now, Dylan wondered if Frankie would even remember her. Guilt flushed her veins, and she sat frozen in her seat until a loud thud caused her to jump. "Holy shit, what was that?"

A little girl clawed at her window with bloody fingertips, her teeth bared in a vicious grin. Dylan pressed a trembling hand to her chest, trying to still its frantic beating. The child's snarls filled her ears, and she closed her eyes for a brief second. "To hell with this town. I'm out of here."

Jamming her foot on the gas, she roared away, leaving the zombie child stumbling along in her wake. Three more figures joined it, all trying their best to catch her, but she soon left them behind. Even they were no match for the speed of a car.

Dylan lit another cigarette to calm her shattered nerves, sucking on the filter until her hands stopped shaking. The countryside flashed by her windows, but she paid little heed to it. Her brain kept circling the little girl. Around every zombie she'd seen so far. Soon, she'd be one of them unless she killed herself before she turned.

That wasn't even the worst of it. As the virus progressed, so did the symptoms. While it started as mild flu, it quickly changed into something far worse as the tissues in the body began to bleed at random. The veins blackened until it resembled a road map beneath the skin. Your eyes darkened until they became pitch black and psychotic episodes presented in even the most mild-mannered of people. Many reported increased hunger too. A craving for meat that turned cannibalistic in the end. *And what about Frankie? What if she's one of them? Could I kill her? Shoot her like the zombie at the supermarket? No!*

"That's enough!" With a shudder, Dylan shook her head to rid it of its morbid thoughts. When the time came, she'd do what had to be done. She was strong. A survivor.

Minutes later, she climbed onto the 29 and headed toward

Edinburg. It wasn't far, and she'd reach it soon enough. Behind her, Springfield continued its slow collapse into anarchy. A blanket of smoke covered the city as key installations burned, either through the actions of looters or an accident. Though it had never felt like home, it was still a shame that so much history was being lost: The Abraham Lincoln Presidential Library and Museum, the Lincoln Monument and home...all of it gone.

Just outside of Rochester, a crude cardboard sign announced that fuel was available at the next stop. Dylan eyed the board with mistrust before pulling up to the gas station, wary of a trap.

The place was ancient. Weathered and peeling. A single pump stood in front of the shop with its shuttered windows. She parked next to it and hesitated, one hand resting on her gun. Before she could get out, an old man carrying a shotgun walked through the door and strode over.

He gave her the once-over before nodding. "Looking for gas?"

"Yes, Sir," Dylan replied.

"Got something to trade?"

"You won't take cash?" she asked, thumbing the last few hundred dollar bills she carried in her pocket.

"Cash is of no use to me, Miss," he said.

After a moment's hesitation, she opened her door and climbed out, taking care to hide her bite mark from him. "I've got food in the trunk. I'll give you half of it for a full tank."

"Show me first."

She unlocked the back and revealed the supplies she'd grabbed at the supermarket. They haggled over the contents for a few minutes with Dylan insisting on keeping the water.

31

"You must have some stored away."

"Yeah, alright. Keep the water," he relented at last before carting away his share of the food. After he filled her tank, he shook her hand and stood back. "Be careful, Miss. The world's a dangerous place now."

"It always was," she replied, before driving off in a cloud of dust.

Edinburg was next, but she passed through without mishap by sticking to the quieter roads. The population in this part of the country was sparse, consisting mostly of tiny villages, a definite boon in these awful times. A lot of people had fled their homes too, heading toward one of the many quarantine zones set up by the government. She hadn't bothered. Her trust in the authorities didn't stretch very far, and she imagined the safe zones closely resembled concentration camps. "No, thank you. Not for me."

She found herself enjoying the drive, the quiet roads, and the countryside. It was a definite improvement over her dingy little apartment and the chaos of Springfield. Not long after Edinburg, she rolled into Sharpsburg. It, too, was quiet. The streets deserted and empty. Luckily, she still remembered where Frankie lived and found the house without too much trouble.

It was a typical suburban home, tucked away in a quiet cul de sac and fronted by a fenced garden. The eaves were painted green, the walls white, and the driveway was paved in stone. A beautiful place of the kind Dylan wished she could have grown up in.

Instead, Frankie had. She'd had the loving parents and stable home that Dylan never got to experience. Still, Dylan didn't envy her. When Frankie was barely out of school, her parents died in a car crash. She inherited the house and a sizable chunk of money, but it was never the same, the rooms empty of life and laughter.

Now, as Dylan faced the locked gates, she wondered what waited inside. Was Frankie still alive? Did she even still live there? Dylan took a deep breath and steeled herself. "Only one way to find out."

As she got out of the car, a cold breeze lifted the hair from her neck. Dried leaves swirled around her feet, and shiver worked its way down her spine. Not for the first time, she wished she'd grabbed a jacket on her way out that morning. As she turned to walk toward the gate, Dylan glanced at her watch and blanched. *Sixty-nine hours, forty-two minutes, and ten seconds remaining.*

Chapter 6 - Dylan

Dylan tested the gate with a tentative hand. It was locked. There was no bell to ring. No buzzer or intercom, and calling Frankie was out of the question. The networks had crashed days ago, and standing around in the open made her a target for any passing undead.

"Here goes nothing," she muttered before climbing over. Her feet landed on the ground with a soft thud, and she pulled out her gun, just in case. "Let's see if anyone's home."

With all her senses on high alert, she made her way to the front door. Along the way, she cast her gaze across the garden, noting that the grass was knee-high and the flowerbeds were overgrown. That didn't mean her friend wasn't there, though. Gardening wasn't exactly a top priority during the apocalypse.

Dylan reached the front porch and walked up the steps with slow deliberation. She wasn't at all sure she was ready for this. The thought of Frankie jumping out at her as a zombie was almost enough to make her turn around and flee.

She peered through the stained glass on either side of the wooden door. It was a wasted effort, however, for she couldn't see a thing. Dylan flexed her fingers and reached for the brass knob. The door swung open with a loud creak, and she jumped back with her weapon held ready. Her heart thudded painfully in her chest as she waited for something to leap at her. Several seconds passed, and nothing happened.

With a sigh of relief, she cast a last look around the neighborhood before stepping inside. The air smelled musty, and the interior was dim, the curtains drawn. Plumes of dust puffed up around her boots with each step she took, teasing her nostrils. Nobody had cleaned in a long time.

A sneeze threatened to erupt, and she paused to gain control of herself first. Once her eyes stopped watering, she called out in a tentative voice. "Frankie? Are you in there? It's Dylan."

Not a soul stirred.

By now, she was sure the house was deserted.

"Guess it's just me then." Disappointment filled her chest, and she glanced back at her car. What was the point in investigating further? Her friend was gone. But maybe, Frankie had left a clue as to her whereabouts. It was a long shot, but... "What else am I going to do?"

She flicked on a light, gratified to see the power was still on. Despite the failing infrastructure and lack of communications systems, the grid was still holding in most places, providing water and electricity. But for how long was anybody's guess.

As she moved through the house, step by step, Dylan was gripped by a strong sense of deja vu. She'd only been inside the place once, a week after Frankie's parents died in the car crash. They'd had the memorial there, and as Frankie's best friend, she'd attended.

On that day, the rooms had been filled with grieving family and friends. People spoke in hushed whispers while sipping on cups of tea. Frankie had looked beautiful but pale in her black dress, accepting an endless stream of condolences. At one point, she'd disappeared, and Dylan found her in the master bathroom, sobbing into a towel while holding a razor blade. The memory thrust its way into the forefront of Dylan's mind, insisting on being relived.

***

"Oh, Frankie. Not that. Anything but that," Dylan cried, grabbing the blade from Frankie's cold fingers.

"It hurts so much," Frankie said, her eyes puffy and swollen. "I want it to stop."

"Oh, sweetie. It will stop...in time," Dylan said, gathering Frankie into her arms.

"I want it to stop now," Frankie cried, her voice muffled against Dylan's shoulder.

"I know," Dylan said, rocking her friend back and forth as she cried. "I know."

***

The memory faded, though its after-effects remained, and the air felt laden with misery. Dylan cleared the foyer, living room, and the kitchen before moving on to the dining room. She briefly debated going upstairs but decided against it. The place was abandoned, and it felt like a violation of Frankie's privacy.

A denim jacket hung on the back of a chair. She tucked away her gun before shrugging it on, grateful for the warmth. A whiff of musk teased her nose, and she buried her face in the collar. It still smelled of Frankie and the perfume she used to wear.

Suppressing her feelings, Dylan forced herself to keep looking for clues, and her eyes fell on a bundle of papers strewn across the dining room table. She moved closer and brushed away the accumulated dust with one hand.

It was a map.

A map covered in sticky notes.

Intrigued, Dylan leaned closer.

On the map itself, Sharpsburg was circled in red. A long, wriggly line ran down from it, following a route across the border of Illinois and into Kentucky. It ended at Fort Knox next to Radcliff which was likewise marked with red. She frowned. "It looks like Frankie was planning a trip to Fort Knox, but why?"

After scanning the sticky notes, the answer became clear. In order, they read:

"Fort Knox, safe zone."

"Stick to back roads, avoid heavily populated areas."

"Distance approximately three hundred miles."

"Five and a half hours drive if all goes well."

Next to the map lay a paper with a long list of supplies written on it, a mixture of food, water, medical items, and so forth. Dylan nodded to herself, leaning against the table. "She was heading for safety, and what better place than Fort Knox?"

During the early days of the outbreak, the government had set up several quarantine zones. Some, like Fort Knox, were large and meant to protect both citizens and essential installations. Others were small, set up in community centers and such. A lot of people viewed these sites as their salvation, but just as many elected to stay home and ride it out on their own, Dylan among them. Apparently, Frankie had decided to head to Fort Knox.

On the one hand, Dylan was glad Frankie had headed to a secure facility. It meant she'd survived the initial outbreak, and hopefully, the trip as well. "But what about me? I can't go. No one in their right mind would accept a sick person into their midst."

Dylan stared at the wound on her arm. Already, it showed signs of infection. The area was red, swollen, and hot to the touch. In a sudden fit of rage, she swept the map of the table, sending papers flying all over the room. "Why me? Wasn't my life shitty enough before all this happened?"

Hot tears burned her eyelids, a mixture of rage and despair. After everything she'd been through, after all the years of fighting to survive a system that tried to crush the life out of her, it came down to this. Dying a horrible death because of one stupid mistake. "Fuck!"

Dylan turned away from the table and headed toward the front door. There was nothing for her here now. No hope, no safety, no friend. Nothing but a slow death in a house that didn't belong to her. "I'm leaving."

Her boot came down on a piece of paper and slid out from underneath her. Teetering for balance, she lost the fight and crashed to the ground, falling hard. Dylan groaned and sat upright, rubbing her bruised lower back with one hand. "Ow. That hurt."

While she waited for the pain to pass, her eyes fell on the offending bit of paper that had caused her fall. It was yet another sticky note covered in Frankie's looping handwriting. None of that mattered, though. All that mattered was the single word that stood out from among the rest. *Cure.*

Grabbing the paper, she read and reread the thing until it was burned into her brain with utter clarity: Fort Knox has a cure. Enough time to get Peter there? Day three.

Dylan frowned. "Peter? Who's Peter? And what does she mean by day three?"

Suddenly, she remembered her and Frankie's last conversation, a hasty call made about two months before. Frankie had told her about a new boyfriend, a guy named Peter. Dylan hadn't paid much attention, but Frankie had sounded pretty serious about him. "Was that why she'd planned the trip to Fort Knox? To save him? But if he was on day three already, she was taking a serious risk."

Dylan scrambled to her feet and gathered up all the scattered papers she'd strewn about. She smoothed out the map and looked at the various sticky notes. It was apparent Frankie had planned to take Peter to Fort Knox, hoping to get him there in time for the cure to work. If they encountered no problems along the way, it was possible. Even so, it was dangerous. Day three was marked by psychotic episodes, and a worm of worry for her friend entered Dylan's mind.

At the same time, hope blossomed amidst her fear for Frankie's life. A cure! Not only that, she was only on day one. She had plenty of time to make it. "I can be fixed! I don't have to die!"

Dylan glanced at the watch on her wrist, struck with a newfound sense of urgency. She had just over sixty-nine hours left. "I can do this. I can make it."

She folded up the map and stuck it into her pocket, preparing to leave. As she turned, she bumped into the dining room chair. It toppled over with a loud crash, and she winced at the sound. Moments later, a thump sounded from upstairs.

Dylan froze, wondering if she'd heard right, but the first noise was followed by a second, louder thump. With careful movements, she drew the gun from her holster and walked toward the base of the stairs. Gazing upwards, she jumped when yet another thump followed the second. There was something on the upper floor, and if her instincts proved correct, it was nothing good.

Chapter 7 - Dylan

Turn around.

Just turn around and get out of the house.

Don't look. Never look. It's too dangerous.

It was futile. She knew she'd go. Just like every dumbass in every horror movie she'd ever watched. Only now, she was in their shoes, and the need to know what was making the noises burned in her chest. It could be Frankie. A zombie. Or sick. Maybe trapped. Stuck with her boyfriend, Peter. Another zombie. Either way, she had to know, no matter what the cost.

Dylan stared at the upper landing, her gun held in both hands. Her arms were trembling. Heck, her whole body was shaking. Whatever waited up those stairs scared the hell out of her. Every fiber of her being yelled at her to run. To take the map and get out of there.

But...she couldn't.

Step by slow step, she went up the stairs. Three generations of the family stared back at her along the way, each face framed in a moment that would last forever. The youngest was Frankie. Her blue eyes shining through a mess of blonde curls. Just the way Dylan remembered. *I'm sorry I wasn't there when you needed me. I'm sorry I bailed after your parents' deaths. I'm sorry I couldn't deal with your sorrow.*

None of that mattered as she went up the stairs, clutching her gun with sweaty palms. The landing appeared, the carpet as pristine as snow. Three doors led off the corridor. Each open. At the end, the master bedroom's door loomed. Shut. A single bloody handprint was smeared across the surface, and Dylan swallowed at the sight. "Please, don't let it be Frankie's. Please."

She forced her reluctant body to move, to close the distance. Her nostrils flared as a horrid stench thickened the air, clinging to the back of her throat. Her hand reached out and touched the handle. It turned beneath her palm, swinging inward on creaky hinges. A monster burst through, teeth snapping at her flesh. His eyes were black, same as the veins crossing his skin. A map of death.

Terror surged through Dylan, electrifying her nervous system like a bolt of lightning. She stumbled backward on legs turned to jelly, and her finger tightened on the trigger. The shot went wild, a clean miss. Before she could try again he was on her, knocking her hand aside with such force that the gun went flying.

Dylan leaped for her pistol, desperate to catch it. She missed by a mere inch. It landed with a clatter, skittered across the floor and slipped through the railings, falling to the landing below.

"No!" Dylan cried, running for the stairs.

Peter, or whoever he was, grabbed a handful of her hair and yanked her backward. His strength was incredible, and he pulled her clean off her feet. She landed hard, pain lancing through her back. He gnashed at her exposed throat, and she reacted on instinct, punching him in the nose. His head snapped back, and putrid blood sprayed from his nostrils.

41

Dylan broke free of his hold with a second punch to the neck, and crab walked away from him toward the stairs. She crawled as fast as she could, and the carpet fibers scratched at her exposed skin.

Peter gave chase, launching himself at her with a vicious snarl as she reached the top of the steps. He bowled her over, and they went tumbling head over heels. Dylan didn't know which way was up as she rolled down the stairs, her arms and legs flailing through the air. Her head hit the railing, followed by her shoulders, hips, and thighs. Pain pierced her ribs. Something crunched, but she couldn't tell what it was. Him or her.

She crashed to a stop at the bottom, half-lying on top of Peter. He wriggled like a worm, clawing at her face with hooked fingers. Fighting to keep his teeth out of her flesh, she spotted the Glock a few feet away.

Fueled by desperation, she kicked against the wall and threw herself forward, but Peter had other plans. He latched onto her arm and bit down, chewing like a rabid dog to get through the denim jacket she wore.

Dylan screamed in agony and twisted around. Using her legs, she knocked him aside and crawled across the floor. A small side table rocked when she bumped against it, and a vase almost brained her. She gripped it by the open mouth and swung it at Peter's head with all the force she could muster. It shattered against his temple, showering them both with shards of porcelain.

He hardly slowed down and kept coming instead. His growls sawed into her brain, adding to the fear already threatening to incapacitate her. She spotted a chunk of the vase next to her and grabbed it. With the sharp end, she stabbed at this face, hoping to pierce the brain. Instead, she cut into the skin of his forehead and sliced open her own hand.

"What the hell?" With a scream of frustration, she launched herself at the gun again. As her hand closed around the butt just as Peter grabbed her foot. He yanked her toward his waiting mouth, and she snapped off three shots in quick succession. Plaster rained from the walls, and her ears sang from the reverberations in the confined space.

The third shot found its mark, and his head exploded in a spray of putrid brain matter. Peter slumped to the ground, leaving her gasping for breath. She fell back, spreadeagled on the carpet as all the strength fled her limbs.

For several seconds, Dylan couldn't move, frozen in place as her mind tried to regroup. The intense fear gradually receded, leaving her drained and exhausted. Her head throbbed in time to the beat of her heart, and it ached to move. She prayed nothing was broken, though it was hard to tell when everything hurt as much as it did. Twitching her fingers and toes, she tested her arms and legs. "Seems okay."

With a grunt, she pushed herself upright and smoothed a lock of hair back from her face. A trickle of blood ran down her temple, staining her fingertips red. A deep gash covered the palm of her hand thanks to the piece of porcelain she'd wielded like a knife, and she hissed when she touched the cut.

It took several tries to get to her feet. Finally, she was up, clinging onto the banister for support. Bile pushed up her throat when she spotted Peter's mangled skull, and she turned away to vomit up her breakfast. It splattered onto her shoes, creating a vile mess.

A low moan and a scrape drew her attention back to the second floor of the house, and a lump formed in her throat. "Frankie?"

43

The word escaped as a broken whisper, and Dylan shook her head, unwilling to face the facts. Her feet began to move of their own volition and carried her up the stairs. Her hand hung at her side, dripping blood onto the carpet. On top of the landing, she paused as her eyes fixed on a horrible sight. It was Frankie, all right. Or what was left of her, at least.

Dylan smothered a sob. "Oh, Frankie. What did he do to you?"

Frankie growled and reached for Dylan with one hand. The other arm ended at the elbow, and her lower body was missing. She dragged herself forward a few more inches, leaving a trail of slime behind. Only her blonde hair was still recognizable.

"I'm so sorry, Frankie. I should've come here sooner. I could've saved you," Dylan whispered as she raised the gun. Time slowed as she gazed into Frankie's eyes, saying goodbye to the girl she'd once known. The blast seemed extra loud to Dylan, and her ears sang as she sank to her knees, dropping the pistol. "I'm sorry."

Dylan sat for a long time, mourning her best and only friend. She remembered all the good times they'd had, and all the bad. The time when Frankie held her hair while she vomited her guts out after a night of heavy partying. The time Frankie came down with measles, looking like a spotty pink balloon. Also, the time that Frankie had asked her to stay, and her expression when Dylan refused, leaving her behind to move on to bigger, better things. Or, so she'd thought.

Now Dylan realized the real reason she'd run. Because she was afraid. Afraid of caring about someone other than herself. It made her vulnerable, and so she'd cut the ties before she could get hurt. A coward's tactics.

Finally, she looked at the ticking time bomb on her wrist and forced herself to stand up. She couldn't save Frankie, but she could save herself, and her friend would've wanted that despite everything.

With tears in her eyes, Dylan wrapped Frankie's remains in a sheet and placed her in her bed. She did the same to Peter but left him downstairs. He was too heavy to drag all the way up steps. After saying a brief prayer for each, she set to work preparing herself for the journey.

She was covered in Peter's blood, and her shoes stank with vomit, so she quickly stripped down and stepped into the shower. In Frankie's cupboards, she found a set of clean clothes: jeans, a flannel shirt, boots, and a jacket. They were the same size, which was a bonus. She also grabbed an extra blanket, a couple of toiletries, and some food and water, stuffing it all into a backpack.

She sported a number of bruises from her fall, and the spot where Peter had bitten her had turned purple, though she was lucky the skin was unbroken. The last thing she needed now was a zombie taking yet another chunk out of her. After disinfecting and bandaging the cuts on her forehead and hand, she rolled up her sleeve and took a proper look at the bite mark on her arm. It was bad. A lot worse than she'd have thought possible in such a short time. Although it felt like an eternity since she'd been to the supermarket, in reality, it was only four hours.

Already it was oozing puss, the area swollen and warm. Black veins radiated outward from the crescent mark like the creeping tendrils of poisonous ivy. While it didn't hurt much, it looked awful.

She cleaned and bandaged the wound while trying to avoid looking at the black veins. They reminded her of Peter and

Frankie, and of what she'd become if she didn't reach Fort Knox in time.

"It's only five and a half hours' drive, and I've got almost a full tank. I can make it," she said, trying to bolster her courage. *If nothing happens along the way.*

She found a bottle of aspirin in a cupboard and swallowed a few, hoping it would help for the fever that would soon set in once the virus got underway. That and the pain from her various cuts and bruises. The rest she tucked into her pocket to take as needed. An energy bar and a bottle of water fortified her for the road, but she only had seven bullets left in her gun. She'd better find more soon or she'd be in real trouble. At least, a baseball bat joined her arsenal, as did a butcher's knife which she tucked into her belt.

Once her preparations were done, she took a last look around. It felt final. She'd most likely never come back again. "Goodbye, Frankie. You were a good friend. A better one than me. Rest in peace."

There was still the problem of getting to her car, however. The neighborhood which had been clear before was now filled with wandering zombies, drawn by the gunshots. After sneaking out of the front door, she made her way to the gate using shrubs and bushes for camouflage.

Once she was as close as it was possible to get, Dylan tossed her bag over the gate. It landed with a thump, and two nearby infected turned toward the sound. With rasping growls, they milled around the lump of canvas looking for food.

"Dumbasses," Dylan muttered while rooting around for a sizeable rock.

She found one and tossed it over the two infected's heads to land in the road with a clatter. Predictably, they rushed over, accompanied by three more that were nearby. After making sure none of the zombies were too close to her, she jumped over the gate, making as little noise as possible. Landing in a low squat, she grabbed her bag and ran to the car.

It was beginning to look like she'd make it without incident when she opened the door. Unfortunately, she'd forgotten about the hinges, and they squealed loudly enough to be heard for miles. As one, every zombie in the vicinity turned toward her, their black-veined, black-eyed faces monstrous to behold.

The closest one charged, and Dylan dropped the bag with haste. Setting her feet apart in a solid stance, she swung the baseball bat at its head. It connected with a hollow thump, and she watched with fascination as his head changed shape from the force of the blow. His skull exploded, and he fell to the ground with barely a whimper.

There was no time to waste, however. More were coming. Dylan pivoted to the left like a dancer and wielded the bat overhead. She slammed it down onto the nearest head like a hammer. The infected, a young woman, fell to the ground with twitching limbs as her eyes rolled back in her skull.

A quick glance around determined that she had a brief second before the next zombie reached her, and she took her chance. Dumping the bat, Dylan grabbed her bag and jumped into the seat behind her. She grasped the handle of the door and pulled.

Just in time.

A zombie thudded into her door and slammed his fists on the window, quickly followed by another and another. Within seconds, she was surrounded, her vision filled with the faces of the undead. Hungry. So, so hungry.

Terror caused her pulse to jump, and she had to concentrate on her movements. Her fingers shook as she started the engine, and she prayed nothing would go wrong. Jamming the car into reverse, she pushed through the crowd and bowled them aside. They howled their frustration as she raced away, putting as much distance between them and herself as she could.

As she left the town behind, Dylan uttered a final farewell. It didn't relieve the hollow pit in her chest, but it needed to be said if she was going to push ahead. "I guess this is it, Frankie. I hope you're with your parents now, and that you're happy. And who knows? Maybe I'll get to see you soon. It all depends on what lies ahead. Goodbye, my friend."

Chapter 8 - Amy

Amy rose before dawn, too restless to sleep any longer. Not that she'd gotten much rest anyway. It was impossible, no matter how tired she was. Ever since she'd buried her mom, things had changed. The house was empty now — a morgue.

Over the past few days, fear had become her constant companion. It grew and grew until it became a thick blanket of paranoia that threatened to smother her. Every night, she'd climb into bed after checking and double-checking all the locks in the house.

She'd clutch the blankets to her chest and stare wide-eyed into the darkness, every little sound a cause for alarm. Her brain would go into overdrive, imagining awful things, until at last, she jumped out of bed more tired than when she got in.

It was a vicious cycle.

Amy yawned as she crossed the hallway to the bathroom, dying to empty her full bladder. The floor was cold beneath her socked feet, and she shivered. "Winter is here, that's for sure."

After using the toilet, she washed up and got dressed before padding downstairs for a quick breakfast. Today, it was cereal and the last bit of milk. The bread was gone already, used for toast the previous morning. She supposed she could try to make more, but she'd never done it before. Her mom had been the baker in the house, spending countless hours producing prize-winning cakes and pies for the local farmers market.

After eating, she poured herself a cup of coffee and sat at the counter, staring into the distance. Her phone lay nearby, but it was useless to her now. There was no signal. No way for her to contact Alex. *Three days. It's been three days.*

Amy shook her head. She didn't want to think about it. It was bad enough losing both of her parents in the space of a week. Not her brother too. She needed him. Needed to believe that he was on his way.

Alex was the perfect older sibling. Strong, kind, and dependable. The sort of brother who protected you from schoolyard bullies and shady boyfriends, but also taught you how to throw a punch. The type who picked you up when you fell, but told you that crying was for sissies.

She missed him more than she could say. Older than her by six years, he'd enlisted in the army right after school. It was his dream, but to her, it meant she rarely got to see him anymore. *Don't worry. He's coming back. He has to be.*

Amy took another sip of her coffee and grimaced. It was cold. After tossing it down the drain, she picked up the shotgun, unlocked the front door, and stepped out onto the porch. The farm stretched out before her, barely visible in the pre-dawn light.

It wasn't much. Just a small patch of fenced land out in the Kentucky countryside. It was nothing like the celebrated horse farms that abounded in the area, but to her parents, it had been heaven. Her father had been an accountant for a firm in Louisville, but he loved nothing more than coming home to the quiet of the farm. Her mother enjoyed being a stay-at-home mom. She raised chickens, grew her own vegetables, baked delicious pastries, and made her own marmalade. It was a simple life, but they'd been happy, and so had Amy.

Amy loved the lush green fields and the patches of forest where wildlife abounded. Though she often went out hunting, she rarely killed anything, preferring to observe the animals instead. She was a good shot, however. Almost as good as Alex.

Now that her parents were gone, and it was up to her to keep the place running. With that in mind, Amy set about completing her chores for the day. It might be the apocalypse, but the chickens still needed feeding, and the vegetable patch wouldn't weed itself.

Ham, the rooster, strutted past when she approached. He was getting ready to wake the dead with his morning song. Amy snorted and tossed him a handful of seed before turning to the hens.

They clucked around her feet while she gathered their eggs, a bounty she was thankful for now more than ever. That, and the vegetable plot. At least, she'd have fresh produce to relieve the monotony of canned goods.

After feeding them and topping up the water trough, Amy eyed the hens with a shrewd gaze. Come Thanksgiving their fat, and feathered bodies would yield a juicy meal. A sudden thought occurred to her, and she frowned. "Will I still be here then? And what about Christmas? What if Alex doesn't come back?"

A fit of panic overcame Amy, and she sank to her knees. Her heart fluttered like a frightened rabbit, and black spots danced in front of her eyes. She pressed her trembling hands to the earth and tried to ground herself.

Oblivious to her fears, the chickens carried on with the

business of eating. They pecked at the earth with laser precision, never missing a seed or a worm. She found their gentle clucking strangely comforting and couldn't help but smile at their antics. One pecked at her fingers, and she shooed it away as she got back to her feet. "Scram."

In the background, Ham began his warbling cry to welcome the dawn, and the first rays of the sun peeked over the top of the barn roof. She tilted her face upward to catch its soothing warmth on her skin. It eased away the panic, and Amy faced a simple truth. She was alone, at least until Alex arrived, and there was no guarantee that he ever would. It was up to her whether she lived or died. The time for crying was over.

With a sigh, she got to her feet, cradling the shotgun with one arm. "Well, there's a lot of work to be done. Better get started."

Throughout the morning, Amy busied herself with various chores. She boarded up the ground floor windows, reinforced the doors, and chopped a load of firewood for the fireplace. Cold weather was coming, and she'd best be prepared for it. "Right. What's next? The barn."

With a pen and clipboard, she took stock of the interior. There was a full tank of fuel, a generator hooked up to the house, her mother's car, gardening equipment, as well as a large bin of chicken feed. After jotting it all down, she locked the doors with a thick chain and padlock, securing the supplies against possible marauders.

With her hands on her hips, Amy surveyed the yard. Her eyes fell on the chicken coop, and she noted the sagging wire that barely clung to the frame. "Mm. That won't do. What if a predator comes along? Or a zombie?"

Throughout the rest of the afternoon, she worked on the

coop, replacing the old rusted wire and fixing the gate. She tackled the veggie patch as well. With a basket on one arm, she harvested the last of the summer crop and rooted out any weeds that threatened the winter vegetables.

It was back-breaking labor, but the constant activity kept her mind off her loneliness. It also allowed her to have renewed faith in Alex. He was both strong and resourceful, plus he never broke a promise. "He'll come home. I know it."

Finally, the sun began to dip toward the horizon, and she was ready to call it a day. Her back hurt, and her hands were blistered and bleeding. Still, she felt a deep sense of satisfaction that triumphed over any discomfort she suffered.

Amy headed toward the house. It welcomed her back with familiar arms, warm and cozy after the chill wind outside. Her stomach rumbled, and she whipped up a quick supper of canned spaghetti and meatballs with a green salad. She even prepared a batch of dough using one of her mom's recipes. Come morning, she'd pop it in the oven and hopefully have freshly baked bread for breakfast. The mere thought had her salivating.

Clipboard in hand, she made a list of all the food in the house. There was enough to last her three months or more if she was careful. Her mom had believed in buying bulk, and there were several jars of jams, pickles, and preserves too. The freezer was full of meat and frozen vegetables, a bonus assuming the power lasted. It was still on for the moment, and she hoped it stayed that way.

The real problem she faced was with everyday stuff like milk and butter, but she could probably make do without it. The toilet paper would run out soon, however. She also couldn't count on the water to keep running. On a whim, she grabbed every empty container in the house and filled it with water, just in case. "That's better."

The entire time she worked, she made sure to keep quiet. All the curtains were drawn, and she didn't use the lights, preferring a candle instead. The farm might be fenced, but she wasn't about to announce her presence to the entire world. Zombies weren't the only things that went bump in the night.

Once she'd eaten, she washed the dishes, took a bath, and curled up in front of the tv with an old movie. She didn't try any of the channels. They'd stopped broadcasting a few days ago. Tucked underneath a blanket, she felt secure in the knowledge that the windows were boarded up and the doors locked.

She was halfway through the movie, however, when the chickens began to kick up a fuss. Even Ham carried on, something he never did except at dawn. Something was bothering them, and she hoped it was just a wild critter.

With a frown, Amy got off the couch and reached for the shotgun. It was never far from her side these days. She peered through a gap in the boards that covered the windows overlooking the yard. It was dark outside. Too dark to see anything.

The chickens were going crazy, though, and Amy knew she had to do something besides cower inside the house. With her heart in her throat, she flicked on the porch light. The bright light flooded the yard, and she spotted the figure of a man clawing at the wire of the chicken coop. He growled like a dog and didn't seem to know how to open the door to the coop, luckily for the chickens.

Amy gasped, her worst fears realized. It was a zombie. It had to be. As if he sensed her presence, the man swiveled toward the house and cut across the lawn. The light fell across his diseased face, and she nearly fainted. It was the first time she'd seen an infected up close, and it was far worse than she'd imagined.

His eyes were pits of darkness, and his waxen skin was covered in black veins that looked like poisoned ivy to her panicked brain. There was something wrong with his leg too. The knee was shattered, and pieces of bone shone through the flesh like ivory splinters. They ground together when he walked, but he didn't appear bothered by it or seemed to feel any pain.

Amy squeezed her eyes shut and looked away. It was too much. She couldn't face the horror that shuffled toward her house with such dogged determination. That wasn't a man. That was a monster. How could she fight against something like that? It was impossible. *Maybe if I keep quiet, it'll go away.*

The grinding of bone on bone grated on her nerves. The zombie was getting closer. A low rasp issued from its throat with each step it took. It slowed when it reached the porch steps, but didn't stop. It knew she was there, and it was coming to get her.

Suddenly, Amy's eyes snapped open. She was no coward, and this was her home. She'd be damned if she let anything ruin it. What would Alex say if he found her hiding in the attic like a little girl?

With that thought in mind, she quickly unlocked the door and yanked it open. With one swift move, she pumped the fore-end to load a shell and raised it to her shoulder. The zombie spotted her and snarled, its teeth bared and glinting in the light. Congealed blood covered its shirt, and the smell of death emanated from it. It had fed recently.

Bile rose up Amy's throat, and her stomach convulsed. Before her courage could run out, she aimed at the infected man's head and pulled the trigger. She knew she had to destroy the brain. That much she'd learned from the news broadcasts before they stopped airing.

The powerful shotgun blast knocked the zombie backward. It went flying off the porch to land in the dust where it lay twitching. Amy watched with bated breath until she was sure it was dead.

After a few seconds, she took a few steps forward to get a closer look. The man's face was unrecognizable. A mass of blood and bone. This time, Amy couldn't stop her stomach from revolting, and her entire supper ended up on the ground.

When the heaving finally stopped, she fled back into the house. With trembling hands, she locked the door behind her and sagged to the floor. She'd killed a man. A person. He was infected, she knew, but still a human being. In the morning, she'd have to get rid of the body. Her stomach churned at the thought. "How am I going to do this?"

The silence had no answers for her.

Suddenly, an awful thought occurred to Amy. What if more zombies came? Too many to kill? And how did that one get in? She was supposed to be safe here. The grounds were fenced…unless there was a gap in the wire.

Amy shook her head, gathering up the shreds of her courage. "I'll check it in the morning. I have to. I can't let any more of those things get in, or I could be overrun."

With her decision made, she set off for bed, even though she knew she wouldn't be able to sleep. She had to try, at least. She couldn't afford to let fear get the best of her anymore. "Come on, Amy. You're a fighter. Remember that."

Chapter 9 - Alex

Alex frowned when he spotted the obstruction on the highway. He eased up on the throttle and slowed to a stop. With one boot planted on the asphalt and the bike engine idling in the background, he studied the road ahead.

A multiple vehicle pile-up blocked the way forward. The mangled wrecks of cars, trucks, and even a bus was visible, and Alex swore under his breath. "Damn it. This is the last thing I need right now."

He was already late. He'd told his mom he'd take no more than a couple of days to get home. Instead, the journey had been far more complicated than he'd thought and fraught with danger. Today was day three, and he still had about two hundred miles to go to reach Louisville. While that didn't sound like much, he'd learned a thing or two over the past few days. Ordinarily, he'd be home in two hours tops, but now that same distance could take days.

Alex eased his weight back into his seat. He was in no rush to move forward. The pile-up appeared natural — a genuine car crash caused by the times. But appearances could be deceiving.

For one thing, he couldn't spot any movement among the vehicles, and that was unusual. Crashes like these tended to draw infected like moths to a flame. Not only that, but the victims themselves could often be found either trapped in their cars or wandering about like ghosts in a daze. He'd seen a lot of that, and each time it tore at his heart. He helped where he could and shot his way through when he couldn't. It was the best he could offer, and it never felt like enough.

Here, there was nothing like that. No infected, no victims, no movement at all. It didn't feel right. Something about this blockade bothered him, and he thought back over the past three days and everything he'd been through to get here.

It was a lot.

After acquiring his new ride, he'd left Kansas City like his tail was on fire. By that time, it was already late afternoon, and after traveling for an hour, he had to concede defeat. Riding blind at night was not a good idea, so he holed up in an abandoned barn. That wasn't so bad. He had food and water, after all, and managed to keep warm by building a small fire.

The next morning, he set off again after filling up his gas tank. He was convinced he'd be home soon, but fate had other plans. In Columbia, someone tried to steal his bike while he topped up on supplies. He'd been lucky to return in the nick of time, or he'd have lost his ride.

St. Louis was a war zone, and he barely escaped with his life. It was only the bike that saved him by allowing him to zip through small spaces, cut across parks, and jump pavements. Even worse, he lost both his jerry cans there and had to push ahead with only half a tank. Not long after that, the gas ran out, and he had to push the bike until he could scavenge more fuel from abandoned cars. That slowed him down considerably, and he spent the second night camped up in a tree — an experience he wouldn't wish on his worst enemy.

He'd seen a lot along the way too. Things he wished could be unseen. The collapse of law and order meant that the worst of the worst had free rein, and the ugly side of humanity was laid bare. Looting, raping, and murdering was common. Throw a couple of million zombies into the mix, and you had a full-blown apocalypse on your hands.

Alex sighed, returning his attention to the pile-up in front of him. It covered the entire road, offering no way through except for a small gap to the left that looked inviting. Easy.

Too easy.

"Ambush?" Alex wondered. It was possible. More than possible. Likely even.

One hand tapped restlessly against his leg as he considered his options. Turning back wasn't possible, but neither did he want to get robbed, killed, or both.

"Do the unexpected. Take them by surprise," he muttered, eyeing the right side of the road. It appeared to be impassable.

To a car, at least.

But not his bike.

Maybe, just maybe, he could cut through the trees and make his escape without triggering the trap that he was sure lay waiting ahead. He had guns, of course, but would rather avoid a firefight if he could.

With a curt nod to himself, Alex took a deep breath. "Here goes nothing."

He closed the visor of his helmet and rode forward at a slow pace, angling toward the left side. The easy side. His heart hammered in his chest, and his mouth was dry. At any moment, he expected bullets to come flying his way. It took every bit of self-control he had not to turn around and race away. "Come on, Alex. You can do this. It's for Amy, remember that."

Alex kept the bike on course for as long as he could, keeping to an even speed. The pile-up grew closer and closer. His eyes roved across the smashed up vehicles and twisted steel. Still no movement. No sign of people.

At the last moment, he swerved away from the enticing opening on the left and raced toward the other side. He pushed the bike to the max, changing gears with lightning speed. He reached the far edge of the barricade and hit gravel where the tar ended. A sharp turn to the left nearly proved his undoing as the tires slid on the loose dirt. Stones flew in every direction, and he kicked out with one leg to regain his balance.

By some miracle, he managed to stay upright and shot forward. The going was rough with shrubs, trees, and clumps of grass clogging the way. Alex maneuvered as well as he could, swerving around tree trunks and dodging bushes as he forged ahead.

A spatter of gunfire sounded, and a bullet clipped a tree in front of him. It zinged off into the distance and confirmed his suspicions. *Ambush.*

More shots kicked up plumes of dirt around him, and he hunched down onto the bike to present a smaller target. A man reared up from behind a shrub holding a hammer and yelled, "Stop right there!"

Alex didn't slow, nor did he turn away. Instead, he headed straight for the guy, passing right by him. At the same time, he kicked out with his right foot and landed a hard blow to the chest. The man dropped the hammer and fell as his breath left his lungs in a loud oof.

With a quick turn of the handlebars, Alex shot around the corner of the barrier and ramped over a slight rise in the ground. He hit the tar road with both tires, his knees braced for the impact.

A blonde woman wearing a startled expression jumped up from her crouched position. She leveled her pistol at him and pulled the trigger. Alex ducked, his entire body seizing up in expectation of a bullet hitting his flesh. Instead, the shot clipped the front fender. The bike wobbled from the force of the hit, and the back wheel began a sideward slide from which there was no return. "Shit!"

Alex fought to regain control but failed. At the last moment, he kicked off into the air, performing a flying leap straight at the woman. Her expression changed from startled to horrified, and she raised both hands to fend him off.

He hit her with incredible force, and they both went tumbling across the road. His arms and legs spun like a top until he came to a grinding halt. With a groan, he raised his head to look around. An experimental twitch of each limb showed him nothing was broken.

The woman hadn't been quite as lucky. She'd hit a nearby car wreck and lay slumped against it like a rag doll. Her eyes were wide open and unseeing, her head bent at an unnatural angle.

"Broken neck," Alex muttered, removing his helmet to allow for a clear field of vision.

Movement caught his eye, and Alex spotted a figure running toward him from the far side of the blockade. He hunched down next to the dead woman and unslung his carbine, ready to shoot. He was caught off guard when his attacker leaped across the hood of the car, landing almost on top of him.

Alex tried to roll aside, but his assailant was fast. Steel flashed in the man's hand, and he struck with the speed of a rattlesnake. Alex grunted as the blade slid home, cutting deep into his side. White-hot agony shot through his torso. He twisted free and delivered a chopping blow with his rifle stock. It connected with his attacker's jaw, hard enough to break bone. Blood and spit sprayed from between broken lips, and the man dropped to the ground with a pained cry.

Alex whipped his gun around and shot him in the chest, putting him down for good. Heaving for breath, he slumped against the car as another hail of bullets cut through the air above his head.

By the sound of things, there was only one shooter left. A glance over his shoulder showed no signs of the guy he'd kicked earlier. Hopefully, he'd either run off or was too badly hurt to come at Alex again. This didn't look like a very sophisticated set-up — just a bunch of wannabe bad guys robbing unsuspecting travelers.

He waited for a lull in the shooting before daring to take a look. Like a real amateur, the other shooter had emptied his gun and was now reloading in plain sight.

"Dumb ass," Alex muttered.

He lined up his sight and squeezed off a shot. Bulls eye. The third attacker's head whipped back. He crumpled to the ground, dead before he hit the tar.

Alex allowed himself a nod of satisfaction. He didn't relish killing people, but this lot had asked for it, preying on the weak like a flock of vultures. He sighed and pressed one hand to his bleeding side. He needed to get to his bike and get himself patched up.

A grunt was the only warning he got. Instinct kicked in, and he jerked his head aside. The hammer whistled past his face and crashed into the side of the car. Metal crunched beneath the solid block of steel meant to stave in his skull. He ducked beneath a second blow that smashed the window above his head, showering him with glass fragments.

"Piece of shit. Killing my friends like that. My girl," the guy roared, bringing the hammer down with brute force.

Alex rolled aside but caught a glancing blow on the upper arm that was enough to make him drop his rifle. He threw himself backward, scrambling across the rough gravel to escape. His shoulder and arm throbbed, pain shooting through the injured limb with each move he made.

"I'm gonna kill you!" Hammer guy kept coming, a hulking behemoth with a thick beard and sagging pants. He swung the blunt head of his weapon with sweeping blows meant to take a man's head off.

Alex was forced to retreat in an awkward scramble across the tar, unable to get to his feet. The hammer smashed into the tar between his legs, and he had a brief vision of being castrated right there and then.

Suddenly, his hand brushed against something solid, and he risked a quick look. It was the woman's pistol. The one she'd dropped when he smashed into her earlier. Hope flared in his breast, and he gripped the butt with fierce determination.

Ignoring the pain in his shoulder, Alex raised the gun and emptied the entire magazine into his attacker's torso. It was overkill, a waste of ammunition, but he couldn't help himself. Primal fear directed his actions. The man was a monster, and he had to go down. Now.

Hammer man stopped mid-swing as the bullets thumped into his chest, one after the other. Nine shots in all. His coal-black eyes fixed on Alex's face, and he hissed. "Stinking piece of shit."

For a moment, he remained standing, swaying gently. Then he toppled over backward and crashed to the ground. His legs twitched for a moment before he lay still. Dead at last.

Alex waited for several seconds, staring at the corpse with caution. He almost couldn't believe the guy was dead. "What a freaking monster."

Slowly, he rolled onto his knees. His breath rasped in and out of his lungs, and sweat dripped from his forehead. The slightest movement caused him to grimace with pain, but he had to move. The shots would draw zombies or even other bad guys.

Alex stumbled toward his crashed bike. To his immense relief, it was intact with no severe damage. It started on the second try, and he sent up a quick prayer of thanks before removing the first-aid kit. He pulled out a splint meant for stabilizing broken bones and placed it beneath his teeth. He was going to need it. Biting down on the hard plastic, he lifted his shirt and examined the knife wound. It was deep — a wide slit in the flesh that seeped blood at a steady rate.

He took a tube of antiseptic salve and pushed the nozzle right into the cut and squeezed. The thick ointment spread throughout the wound, and he kept at it until it oozed from the edges. Satisfied, he slapped a thick wad of gauze onto it and stuck an adhesive bandage over the area. As an added precaution, he wrapped cotton bandages around his midriff to secure it in place with more band-aids. It would have to hold until he got home.

By the time he was finished, Alex was about ready to pass out. His jaw ached from biting down on the splint, and he removed the mangled thing with trembling fingers. "Holy shit, that hurt."

There was no time to waste, though. He had to get away from the area as fast as he could. After swallowing a bottle of water and a couple of aspirin, he looked around. A quick search yielded him an empty pistol, a rifle, a hunting knife, and the hammer that nearly ended his dream of becoming a father one day. He stuck them all into his saddlebags before straddling the seat. "Here goes."

He rode away from the site of the ambush, clinging to the handlebars like a monkey. The vibrations of the engine traveled through his injured middle and caused fiery pain to shoot up his side. His bruised shoulder throbbed in time to the beat of his heart. In no time at all, he had to stop to take a break.

After the third stop, Alex had to face the truth. He wasn't getting home that day. He'd have to spend another night by the side of the road. Two hundred miles was just too far in his current condition, and he'd better start looking for shelter. Plus, he'd have to take the back roads to avoid Louisville. If it was anything like St. Louis, it was no place for him, hurt like he was. On the one hand, it meant a safer journey, but on the other, it would take longer too. "Damn it all to hell. I'm sorry, Amy, but I'll be there soon. Just hold on."

Chapter 10 - Dylan

Dylan navigated through the streets of Sharpsburg and headed South-East to Taylorville. It was past noon already, and banks of gray clouds had moved in on the horizon. The countryside flashed by her window, its colors muted and dull beneath the sunless sky. An occasional farmhouse showed in the distance surrounded by crops and fields, but she paid little attention to any of it.

Instead, she remembered how the undead had surrounded her at the house and pulled over to transfer her supplies from the trunk to the back seat. Her stomach rumbled, and she ate another energy bar and drank a soda.

After that, she hit the road once more, following the route mapped out by Frankie. It was a good one which avoided the most densely populated areas where possible. With the window open a crack, she lit another cigarette from her small stash and drove as fast as the old sedan allowed.

She made good progress in this manner, passing through both Taylorville and Owaneco without mishap. She slowed down and drove with care, keeping an eye on her surroundings and steering clear of anything that looked like trouble.

The road wasn't empty. There was other traffic. People like her heading for safer climes, maybe looking for something or someone. Once, she spotted a wreck and slowed to investigate. There was blood smeared on the windows, and she wondered if the driver had become a zombie. Anything was possible now.

At one stage, she fiddled with the radio but failed to pick up any stations. Nor had Susan possessed anything in the way of music, so the time passed in absolute silence. She was starting to wish for company when she spotted a woman and child standing next to a stranded car. The woman waved her down, and Dylan pulled over but kept the doors and windows shut. "Can I help you?"

"Yes, please. We need help. Our car's run out of gas," the woman said with a friendly smile. "If you could give us a little, I'd be very grateful."

"I don't have any to spare. Sorry."

"We don't need much. Just enough to get us to the next town, Millersville. It's not far, and we can get more there," the woman replied, her smile becoming strained.

Dylan looked at her fuel gauge and shook her head. She couldn't afford to part with any of her precious fuel. Not if she wanted to make it to Fort Knox. Who knew when she might get the chance to fill up again. "Where are you headed?"

"To Vandalia," the woman replied. "My mother lives there in a gated community. She says it's pretty safe, and I have to look after my son. He's all I've got."

"I can't give you any fuel, but I can give you a lift. It's on my way," Dylan said, eyeing the boy who waved at her through the window.

The woman's shoulders sagged with relief. "You'd take us all the way there? That's so kind of you. Thank you so much."

"It's okay. Just load your stuff into the trunk, and we can get going," Dylan said, popping the back open.

She watched while the boy and his mom transferred their luggage then unlocked the doors to let them in. As the woman slid into the seat next to her, she introduced herself. "My name's Madeline, but everyone calls me Maddie. This is Kyle."

Kyle ducked his head and waved, and Dylan guessed him to be about fourteen. "I'm Dylan. Nice to meet you," she replied. "Buckle up; we've got a ways to go."

As she steered onto the road once more, she couldn't help but glance at her watch.

Sixty-seven hours and counting.

The first few minutes passed in awkward silence. Dylan had no idea what to say to the strange woman sitting next to her, or her son. After a while, she cleared her throat. "There's food and water in the back seat. Help yourselves."

The boy, Kyle, looked at his mom. "Can I, Mom? Please?"

Maddie glanced from Dylan to her son before nodding. "Okay, but don't eat everything, sweetie. It doesn't belong to us."

Dylan suppressed a grin as Kyle tore into the energy bars and sodas, probably the closest he'd gotten to candy in days. His mother chose a bottle of water and a packet of dried fruit, chewing slowly as she stared ahead.

"Thank you for the food," Maddie said after finishing her apricots. "We ran out a day ago, and I've been too scared to stop anywhere to get more."

Dylan nodded. "Don't mention it. Things are pretty crazy at the moment."

"Where are you headed? Have you got a family?" Maddie asked.

"Not me. I'm a foster kid," Dylan replied.

"I'm sorry," Maddie said.

"Don't be. It's not your fault." Dylan longed for a smoke, but a quick look at Kyle munching away in the back seat deterred her.

"What happened to you?" Kyle blurted after eating his third bar in a row.

"What do you mean?" Dylan asked.

"You're covered in bandages," he pointed out. "Plus, your cheek is bruised."

"Don't be rude, Kyle," Maddie admonished.

"It's okay. I don't mind," Dylan said before smiling at Kyle. "I had a run-in with a zombie earlier and got hurt."

Kyle stopped chewing and stared at her with wide eyes. "You fought a zombie? For real?"

Maddie gasped and pulled away from Dylan, pressing her back against the passenger side door. "A zombie?"

Dylan's smile faded. "Relax. I killed it."

Maddie didn't relax. Instead, she looked at Dylan like she'd suddenly turned into a cockroach. "Did you get bitten? Are you infected?"

Dylan stared at Maddie for a second before realizing she'd said too much. Judging by the woman's reaction, she wouldn't take kindly to Dylan being sick with the virus. Not even if she was still on day one. Suddenly, she was very glad her jacket hid the bandage and black veins on her arm. "No. I'm not infected. I got hurt trying to get away from him."

"Are you sure?" Maddie asked with narrowed eyes, her voice thick with suspicion.

"Yes, I'm sure," Dylan said, pointing at her head and hand. "I got this while falling down the stairs, and this while stabbing the zombie with a piece of pottery. The bruises come from the stairs too. I took quite a tumble."

"How can I trust you?"

"I guess you can't," Dylan replied, fighting to remain calm. "But this is my car, and you're welcome to walk the rest of the way if you wish."

"I…" Maddie's mouth worked, searching for words.

Kyle chipped in, a worried frown marring his forehead. "Mom, she's fine. Look at her. She's not turning into a zombie. I've heard it takes days anyway."

"Listen to your son," Dylan advised. "It's a long way to Vandalia on foot. But by car, you'll be there within an hour. Safe and sound."

"I suppose you're right," Maddie said after a tense few seconds. With slow movements, she slid back into her seat, though her stiff shoulders betrayed her mistrust.

Dylan sighed, already regretting her kindness of earlier. *This is going to be the longest drive of my life.*

Chapter 11 - Dylan

They drove in silence until they hit Millersville. As they neared the town, Dylan spotted a cloud of smoke hanging above it. Worried about what they might find, she slowed the car to a crawl.

Maddie tensed up again, a deep furrow forming between her brows. She gripped the dashboard and asked, "What's going on?"

"I don't know — something's burning. Keep your eyes open," Dylan said. "You too, Kyle."

The boy nodded and gazed out the window with serious intent as they cruised between the buildings while sticking to the main road. It was mostly deserted except for a few cars parked along the side, and it looked almost normal. They'd nearly passed through the town when Kyle spotted the origin of the fire. "Over there!"

Dylan edged closer, slowing down even further as her eyes met a strange sight. People armed with all sorts of weapons ranging from guns, pitchforks, sharpened sticks, and shovels were gathered in a small park. The park fronted a large square building made from exposed brick. Its windows and doors were barricaded from the outside and written across the front in dripping white paint were the words: The Infected are

Damned.

Flames licked across the walls, and smoke billowed from the shattered windows. The heat was intense, so strong that Dylan could feel it against her skin all the way across the park.

"What are they doing?" Kyle asked.

"I'm not sure," Dylan said, but a suspicion was forming. The fire, the message, the crowd...it all pointed to one thing.

"They're burning the zombies," Maddie answered, leaning forward in her seat.

"Zombies?" Kyle asked.

Dylan didn't answer. She watched as the fire consumed the building, filled no doubt with the undead. Then a strange noise reached Dylan's ears through the crack in her window, the sound of multiple voices screaming for help. She jerked upright in her seat, listening harder. "Wait a minute. Those aren't zombies."

Maddie glanced at her. "What do you mean?"

Dylan's stomach churned as the horrifying truth sank in. "They're killing infected people. Not zombies."

Maddie's expression didn't change. "What's the difference?"

"The difference is, those people are still alive. They haven't died yet," Dylan said.

"They're burning people alive?" Kyle cried out. "Just because they're sick?"

"I'm afraid so," Dylan said, staring at the awful sight.

Between the planks nailed across the windows, she spotted a few faces, barely visible through the smoke and flames. Hands scrabbled at the wood with frantic desperation as those that burned inside sought to escape an agonizing death. Her stomach churned as she imagined the horror, the terror, and the pain those poor unfortunates were experiencing.

The people outside felt no mercy. That much was clear. Instead, they cheered at the deaths of what must once have been their neighbors, maybe even friends and family. They were getting rid of what they perceived to be the enemy, an evil in their midst, and in the process, they were becoming that same evil.

Suddenly, the crowd rippled and parted down the middle to reveal a struggling duo. An older woman was dragging a young girl to the front. The girl pleaded with the woman, and tears streamed down her cheeks to drip onto her torn and bloody shirt. "Please, Aunt Lily. Please."

The woman ignored her niece's efforts and addressed the gathered townspeople in a loud voice. "I present to you this thing...this zombie for cleansing."

"No, Aunt Lily! I'm not a zombie. I'm not. I swear," the girl cried, trying to pull free from her aunt's iron grip.

"My niece is gone. She died when the infection entered her bloodstream. You're nothing but an infection in our midst. A living canker that will sow death and destruction on us all. Unless we stop you now."

"No, Aunt Lily. Please, I beg of you," the girl cried as two people grabbed her arms and dragged her toward a smoking pyre in the middle of the park. "Don't do this!"

Flames licked at the wood heaped into a pile, burning brightly, and a bed of coals gleamed at the bottom. A charred corpse lay curled up in the middle, the arms and legs pulled into a fetal position during its final moments.

Dylan watched the entire time with growing horror, unable to believe that ordinary people were capable of such barbarism. Her stomach churned when she realized they were capable of it, and that they fully intended to burn the young girl alive.

Without thinking about it, she undid her seatbelt and reached for the door handle until Maddie stopped her. "Where are you going?"

Dylan stared at her for a second. "I'm going to help that girl."

"You can't. She's infected," Maddie said.

"Maybe, but she's not a zombie yet. She can still think and feel. She's still a person," Dylan protested.

"You can't help her," Maddie insisted. "She's already dead, and those people won't let you interfere."

"I don't care. I have to try," Dylan said, watching as the girl was dragged toward the fire kicking and screaming. "I've got a gun."

"Yeah? So do half of them," Maddie said. "You won't get far."

"My mom's right. They'll burn us too. Let's get out of here," Kyle said, wringing his hands together.

Dylan shook her head, fighting against the truth of Maddie's words. She couldn't let the girl die like that. She had to try and save her. "I can't leave. She's all alone."

"Dylan, please. You can't help her. She's dead already, but we're not. My son...we have to protect my son," Maddie cried, gripping Dylan's forearm with steely fingers.

Dylan looked at Maddie's fingers, wrapped around the very place where her own infection began. Hidden. A secret. *These people...they'd burn me too if they found out. They'd kill me without blinking an eye. Just like that girl. We're alone, the two of us. Alone in this world.*

"Please, Dylan. Think of my son," Maddie repeated.

Dylan blinked, and reality shifted. Maddie was right in a sense. She couldn't help that girl. Not without sacrificing herself and possibly Maddie and Kyle too. She was outnumbered and outgunned. Her voice felt raw when she uttered the words,

"Alright, Maddie. We're going."

Maddie sagged with relief. "Thank, God."

Heads were beginning to turn their way, and Dylan realized they were out of time. No one would welcome them, especially not her. She'd be added to the pile of corpses on that pyre, her flesh charring to ashes as she screamed out her final breaths.

"Let's go," she said.

As she turned the car back toward the main street, the scene being played out in the park reached its final act. The girl was tossed onto the fire without ceremony, a broken doll that was of no use to anyone anymore. She twisted and turned as death licked at her flesh, her hair a fiery torch against the gray skies. A brisk wind whipped the flames into a frenzy and carried her screams to the furthest corners of its reach.

Kyle sobbed, his hands pressed to his eyes to deny the sights before him. His mother watched with a stony expression, and Dylan swallowed as vomit stung the back of her throat. It took everything she had not to pull over and scream out her anger and helplessness at the world. Guilt burned her with its hot touch, much like the flames that had consumed the girl. "I can't believe I left her to die like that. That I did nothing."

"You had no choice," Maddie said with cold finality. "It was her or us."

"I know, but..."

"But nothing. She was infected anyway," Maddie said, causing Dylan to look at her with narrowed eyes. Before she could say anything further, Kyle leaned forward and grabbed his mom's shoulder. "How could they do that, Mom?"

Dylan knew what he was asking. He was pleading for answers that would help him make sense of a terrifying new reality. The knowledge that people could, and often would, do terrible things in the name of their beliefs. She doubted he would get any real answers from Maddie, though, and she was soon proved right.

Maddie turned toward her son shrugged, her face a smooth canvas. "I don't know, sweetie. I guess they were protecting themselves."

"Protecting themselves from what?" he asked. "They could've just locked up all the infected people until they turned before they killed them."

"Calm down, sweetie. Forget about those people. It's over."

"How can you say that?"

"It's not as if they were human beings anymore. They were dead already, and they got what they deserved," Maddie said.

"That girl...she didn't deserve to die like that."

"Remember your father, Kyle. He would've killed us in a heartbeat. The infection changed him and took him away from us. He wasn't your dad anymore, and you know it. Just like that girl wasn't her anymore."

"But he was dead when he tried to hurt us. Mom. A zombie. Before that, he was still Dad," Kyle said.

"No, he wasn't. He was infected just like everybody else. A vicious monster," Maddie said, showing genuine anger for the first time. "Your real father was gone the minute he got bitten, taken over by whatever this disease is."

Kyle stared at his mom with an open mouth before curling into a little ball on the seat. He stared into the distance while holding onto his knees, and Dylan felt awful for the poor kid. Silence fell as Millersville shrank into the distance until soft snores indicated that he'd finally fallen asleep.

Dylan cleared her throat. "Do you really believe that? What you said earlier?"

"Believe what?" Maddie asked.

"That the infected are dead already. That they should be killed like that girl," Dylan said.

Maddie fixed Dylan with cold blue eyes. "Of course, I do. They're nothing but a danger to the rest of us."

"Even if they're still alive? They only change once they die," Dylan said in the mildest tone of voice she could manage.

"It doesn't matter. Once infected with the virus, they're not them anymore," Maddie replied.

"They can still feel pain, you know. They can think and feel, just like you and me," Dylan said.

Maddie flashed her a pitying smile. "They only look human, but it doesn't mean they are. Their souls are gone. The thing that remains behind is a monster that must be killed."

"Even Kyle? What if he gets infected?"

Maddie hesitated, her lips quivering before she nodded. "Even Kyle. If he becomes infected, I'll release him from his suffering."

An angry retort rose to Dylan's lips, but she shut them without saying a word. People like Maddie and those of Millersville were the most dangerous kind in the world. They were worse than serial killers and murderers, rapists and thieves, for they believed themselves to be right.

Instead, she kept quiet, all the time vowing to keep both eyes on her at all times. *The sooner I get rid of her, the better. I feel sorry for Kyle, though. Imagine what she'd do to him if he got bitten. What she'd do to me if she knew I was infected.*

Chapter 12 - Dylan

After Millersville, nobody felt much like talking. Kyle alternated between napping on the back seat or staring at his mother with a grim expression, while Maddie concentrated on the countryside. Now and then she'd flash Dylan a strange look, one that made the latter squirm in her seat.

Dylan was caught between two opposites, pity for Kyle and loathing for Maddie. She prayed the rest of the trip would be uneventful, and that she could get rid of the crazy Madeline without anything else going wrong, but her instincts told her that was highly unlikely.

At least, I have a gun, and she doesn't. As long as I keep an eye on her, it should be okay, Dylan thought, shifting in her seat once more.

As the minutes passed, she became hyper-aware of the bite wound on her forearm. The edge of the bandage stuck out from her sleeve whenever she moved in a certain way, and it was the last thing she wanted Maddie to notice.

The wound itself itched and burned too, and a couple of times she caught herself scratching at the material of her jacket while Maddie watched. The fourth time it happened, she forced a bright smile onto her face and her hand back onto the wheel before saying, "So, you're going to your mother's house in

Vandalia?"

"That's right," Maddie said. "She says it's safe. They've set up a neighborhood watch and everything for the zombies."

"It sounds nice," Dylan said, trying to keep her voice light.

"What about you?" Maddie asked. "Where are you going?"

"To a friend in Kentucky. She lives on a farm, and I reckon it'll be a good bet."

"I see," Maddie answered before resuming her vigil of the countryside.

Dylan suppressed a tense sigh, praying Maddie hadn't noticed anything out of the ordinary. She glanced at the fuel gauge and the odometer. They still had three-quarters left in the tank, and only about thirty minutes to go before they reached Vandalia. *Thank, fuck. I just hope Vandalia hasn't gone to the dogs yet.*

"When was the last time you heard from your mother? What does Vandalia look like with the outbreak?" Dylan asked.

Maddie shrugged. "She called me before the networks crashed. The citizens have set up a kind of militia, and they're patrolling the streets for infected. They're trying to block off the town, build walls and roadblocks."

"Will they let us through?" Dylan asked, worry setting in. She didn't trust homegrown militias. Or mobs. Not after what she'd seen at Millersville.

"I'm sure of it. I've got a letter from my mom with her address and everything on it in my pocket. I grew up there, too. There's nothing I don't know about that place," Maddie said without a hint of fear.

Dylan nodded, hoping she was right. If not, she'd shoot the first bugger who tried to touch her. "Okay. I'll take your word for it."

They'd been driving for another ten minutes when Dylan spotted a three-car pile-up blocking the road. She slowed and maneuvered to the side, hoping to bypass the accident when Kyle tapped the window and said, "Wait! Someone is moving inside that car."

Dylan gritted her teeth and resisted the urge to slam her hands on the wheel. This was exactly the kind of situation she'd hoped to avoid. Another delay. Another few precious minutes lost. "Are you sure?"

"He's right. There is someone inside that car. They might be hurt," Maddie said.

Dylan looked at the light. The sun hung low, and dusk was almost upon them. "It's getting late. We should keep going."

"We can't just leave them," Kyle protested, ever the good Samaritan.

Dylan sighed. "Fine, let's have a look, but we should hurry."

She pulled the car off to the side and got out, one hand resting on her gun. Maddie followed after telling Kyle to stay put.

"But, Mom…" he protested.

"Your mom's right, Kyle. We don't know what's waiting up ahead. Stay in the car," Dylan said.

She glanced at Maddie. "Ready?"

Maddie scouted around before picking up a rock the size of her fist and nodded. "Let's go."

"We should take it slow. This could be a trap," Dylan warned.
"I get it."

They crossed the distance to the accident with slow steps, and Dylan quickly became aware of a few things. The car closest to them was empty. It had taken the brunt of the collision, and all the windows were smashed to bits.

Maddie's shoes crunched across the broken glass before she

squatted down and pointed at a splash of blood. A trail of the crimson liquid led to the driver's side door which yawned open, but there was no sign of anyone. No corpse either.

"The blood is old," Dylan said, noting its blackened and congealed state.

"Yeah, I think the driver got hurt but walked away," Maddie said.

"He or she couldn't have gotten far. Not injured like that."

"Maybe, or maybe someone picked them up," Maddie said. "What about the truck? It looks like there's someone in there."

Dylan moved closer to the vehicle in question and peered into the front. A man lay slumped over the wheel, and she cleared her throat. "Hello? Are you okay?"

It was a dumb thing to ask. The man clearly wasn't okay. Not once you noticed the color of his skin or the blood pooled onto the seat. Old blood.

"Dead?" Maddie asked.

"Yup," Dylan said, swallowing hard. She walked over to Maddie, and together, they circled the truck. The third car had come off the lightest of the three. Its windows were still intact, and overall, it looked fine. Just the front bumper had a dent in it.

The windows were lightly tinted, and Maddie leaned in for a closer look before jumping back. "Whoa! Movement, definitely movement!"

"Let me see," Dylan said, peering through the glass. A lipless apparition smashed its face into the window, hissing at them, and Dylan screamed. "Zombie!"

"I thought so," Maddie said from behind Dylan. "He or she must have turned while driving and caused the accident."

"You're probably right," Dylan said. "Look, its seatbelt is on.

It's trapped."

"Just another monster," Maddie said.

Dylan frowned. There was something in the woman's voice that triggered an alarm bell in her head, and she began to turn.

"A monster like you," Maddie said, swinging her arm.

Dylan caught the blurred movement too late, and a heavy weight crashed onto her head. Her knees buckled, and she fell to the ground with a grunt. The world swam around her as she raised her arms to ward off another blow.

The rock Maddie was using as a weapon landed on her wrist, and pain lanced through Dylan's body. It rendered her hand useless, and she couldn't get a grip on her gun.

Maddie picked it up instead and stepped back, the barrel pointed at Dylan's face. "You're infected. Don't think I didn't notice. It was so obvious, the way you tried to hide it."

Dylan looked at the crazed woman between the runnels of blood that poured across her face. Her lips fumbled when she spoke, the words slurred. "Are you really going to kill me? After everything I've done for you?"

"Shut up. You're a zombie. That's all. A filthy cannibal," Maddie screamed, waving the gun around.

"A zombie who saved your life and that of your son's. You'd have died if I left you there by the side of the road. Killed by real zombies."

"I don't care what you did. The fact remains, you're a monster, and you deserve to die," Maddie said. Her arm straightened, and the cold eye of the gun stared at Dylan with unwavering precision. "Your road ends here."

Dylan grinned, tasting her blood where it pooled on her lips. The taste of copper pennies. "I hope you get eaten by my kind, Maddie. I hope they tear you to pieces, bit by bit, while you scream for the mercy you wouldn't grant to others."

"You won't be there to see it," Maddie said, her finger tightening on the trigger.

Here it comes, Dylan thought.

"Mom, no! What are you doing?" Kyle screamed. He crashed into his mother and wrestled the gun from her fingers, catching her by surprise. "You can't kill her. She saved our lives."

Maddie's face tightened. "Kyle, give me the gun."

"No."

"Kyle!"

"Forget it, Mom. You're not killing her," Kyle said, backing away from his mother.

Maddie's expression changed. It softened, and she reached out a pleading hand. "Kyle, please. She's evil. Infected. We have to kill her before she starts killing others."

Kyle shook his head. "Not like this, Mom. If we do this, then we're worse than the zombies."

"Kyle, please. Be reasonable," Maddie pleaded.

"I won't let you," he insisted, taking another step back.

Maddie threw her hands in the air. "Fine, have it your way."

She marched past her son toward the waiting car, leaving a confused Kyle gaping after her. "Mom? What about Dylan? We can't leave her like this. She's hurt."

"Yes, we can, and we will," Maddie said. "I'm letting her live, aren't I?"

Kyle took a step toward her. "Mom, please."

"Get in the car," Maddie screamed, waving a warning finger at Kyle. "If you don't, I'm leaving you here with her."

Kyle hesitated, his gaze jumping between his mother who'd resumed her march, to Dylan who was fighting to remain upright on her knees. "What do I do?"

Dylan blinked slowly. Her vision was wavering, and black encroached on the edges. "Go with your mom, Kyle."

"What about you?" he asked, tears shimmering in his eyes.

"I'll be okay, I promise," Dylan said.

"But…"

"She's your family, and I can't take care of you. Not now," Dylan said.

"Are you sure?" he asked.

"Yes, just…leave me the gun."

He looked at the weapon and handed it to her without hesitation. "It belongs to you anyway."

"Thanks," Dylan said, taking it from him. "Now go. Before she leaves you here."

Kyle stood still for a split-second before raising his hand in a last goodbye. "I'm sorry."

The next moment, he was gone, and seconds later, Dylan heard the car spin away with a screech of the tires. She shook her head to ward off a wave of dizziness, and warm droplets of blood dripped onto her hands. "I can't stay here. I'm too exposed."

She pushed herself to her feet and leaned against the car, ignoring the zombie scrabbling at the window. It couldn't undo its buckle or open the door, so it wasn't a threat. Still, she was injured and out in the open. There could be others, and night was falling. She had an hour at most.

A growl from the nearby bushes sent a shiver of fear rippling through her veins, and she scanned the vicinity with wide eyes. A second and a third growl sounded off to the right, and Dylan knew she was surrounded.

With adrenalin kicking her into high-alert, she considered her options. She had nowhere to run, couldn't fight in her condition, and didn't have enough bullets anyway. *I need to hide. Now.*

That left the pile-up. The first car was out of the question. Its windows were all smashed. The truck's windows were intact, but its passenger door was wedged shut against the body of the first car. She looked at the vehicle behind her and its zombie driver, hissing with relentless hunger. "You've got to be kidding me."

Chapter 13 - Dylan

Dylan opened the back door of the car a crack, gagging when a waft of putrid air hit her nostrils. "Holy shit, that's rank."

The thought of spending the night inside that vehicle with its stench of death and decay was enough to make her want to vomit, but another rustle of bushes spurred her on. She slipped inside and closed the door with a soft click. Through watery eyes, she scanned her surroundings. The incoming infected had yet to show themselves, but she knew they were there and could only pray they hadn't seen her first.

The zombie trapped in the front seat was going nuts, twisting and turning as it tried to grab her with its claw-like hands. She couldn't risk using the gun and pulled the kitchen knife from her belt instead. The same one she'd taken from Frankie's house.

With one hand steadying her against the roof of the vehicle, Dylan stabbed the zombie through the eye, driving the blade deep into its skull. It stiffened for a second, before slumping into its seat with a final groan. Dead at last.

Dylan fell back as another wave of dizziness hit her, made worse by the awful smell, and she pressed one palm against the gash in her scalp. It bled profusely, dripping onto her clothes and running down her face. *I have to stop the bleeding.*

With trembling hands, she removed her jacket and shirt. The shirt had long sleeves which she cut off using the knife. Another piece from the hem formed a thick pad which she pressed to the wound. Hissing with pain, she wrapped the sleeves around her head and tied them off beneath her chin. It was the best she could manage under the circumstances.

With the last of her strength, she dry swallowed two painkillers from the bottle she'd tucked into her pocket earlier and lay back, closing her eyes. The darkness was calling to her, pulling her down into the abyss. With her jacket pulled over her head, she surrendered, falling into a deep, dreamless sleep.

From the roadside bushes, a figure emerged, dark and crooked. It was followed by several more, and they shuffled across the road toward the pile-up on uncertain legs. The smell of fresh blood lay thick in the air, tempting them with its promise of sustenance. They groaned with longing as they searched for their elusive prey, circling around and round the cars. Their shadows fell across the prone figure of Dylan, slumped in the backseat. Fingertips brushed the glass next to her face.

***

A bright shaft of sunlight cut through the slumber that had Dylan in its grip, and she blinked against the glare in her eyes. Her eyes were fuzzy, and her mouth as dry as bone. She worked her jaws and looked around. "What the hell? Where am I, and what's that smell?"

She pushed herself upright only to fall back again with a cry. Her head throbbed, and the slightest move caused stabbing pains to shoot through her skull. "Man, that hurts. Mother effin hell, it hurts."

A wave of nausea rolled over her like a freight train, and

a cold sweat broke out on her forehead. The corpse in the front seat mocked her with its lipless grin, and the smell of its decaying flesh coated her tongue like slime. She twisted to the side and hurled up the contents of her stomach, little though it was. The pain in her head intensified from the pressure, and she nearly blacked out again.

Dylan muffled a sob and curled into a ball, willing the agony away. After half an hour, it faded to a dull throb. Painful, but manageable. Barely.

She sat upright again, moving slowly this time. The sun was bright and sat high in the sky. At least, it wasn't cold. She hated the cold. "That bitch, Maddie. If I get a hold of her, I'm going to strangle her scrawny neck."

Then her eyes fell on her watch, and she gasped. "What's the time?"

It was past eight in the morning already, and she swallowed hard as fear threatened to consume her. She'd lost nearly twelve hours passed out in the back seat of the car. *Twelve hours!* "I've got to get moving. Now."

Dylan reached for the door handle, but reared back when a zombie smashed its face into the window. It swiped at the glass with furious rage, its teeth bared. Two more closed in, banging their fists against the windows, and the fragile material groaned beneath the force of their blows.

Panic set in, and she covered her head with her arms, screaming with helplessness and pain. Her brain refused to work, to function. She was no longer a thinking human being, but mere prey, trapped by a superior predator. "Go away!"

But the zombies didn't go away. If anything, their efforts intensified. A tremor ran through her muscles, and Dylan realized she had to do something fast before she grew too weak. Loss of blood and dehydration had taken its toll, and it would only get worse the longer she waited.

Wiping away the tears, she pulled her gun from its holster. Seven bullets. That was all she had. "Better make it count then."

Leaning over, she wound the window down a crack. When the infected thrust its face into the gap, she shot it through the head. It fell away, replaced seconds later by another. She repeated the procedure until all three zombies were down before allowing herself a moment of optimism. "Please tell me that's the last of them."

After a thorough examination of the outside area, it appeared it was. Still, she had to move before more were drawn by the gunshots. Not that she knew where they were coming from in the first place. A farm, maybe? Stranded cars? Who knew?

Getting out of the car took at least two tries. Her legs were wobbly, and the world spun like a top whenever she moved too fast. Finally, she was out and considering her options. Walking was out of the question. She needed a car.

Her eyes fell on the vehicle in which she'd spent the night. It was the only one of the three that didn't look too badly damaged. Maybe, she was lucky, and it still ran. Wrinkling her nose with disgust, she opened the door and undid the dead zombie's seatbelt before pulling it out onto the asphalt.

It looked as bad as it smelled, and she vomited twice more during the procedure. After sending up a quick prayer, Dylan attempted to start the engine. It took on the third try, and she almost cried with relief. "Thank, God!"

She carefully reversed out of the pile-up and checked the fuel. There was half a tank left, enough to keep her going for a while. A quick search of the trunk delivered an old rag that she used to wipe the wheel and cover the seat, soaked as it was in bodily fluids.

The truck had nothing of use inside it, but the smashed car held a suitcase in the back, and she loaded it into her vehicle without wasting a second. The original owner no longer needed it. Though she was dying to check out the contents, she had to get out of there first. "No telling how many more zombies are hanging around here."

As she drove away, Dylan checked the timer on her wrist once more. The news wasn't good. *Forty-eight hours and twelve minutes remaining.* "Perfect. Just fucking perfect!"

Chapter 14 - Amy

The next morning, Amy dug another hole. This one she placed in a distant corner of the yard, as far away from the house as she could manage. It took hours, but she finally managed to make the grave deep enough. Luckily, the ground was soft due to a bout of recent rain.

After wrapping the corpse in an old blanket, she dragged it toward the hole and dumped it inside. Once the grave was covered with fresh dirt, she uttered a quick prayer for the poor man's soul. Whatever he might have been in death, he was still a person before that: someone's dad, husband, son, or brother. A proper burial was the least she could do for him. "I'm sorry I killed you, but I had no choice, mister. I hope you rest in peace."

With most of the day already gone, she knew she had to hurry. Armed with the pistol, shotgun, a roll of wire and clippers, she set off to patrol the fence. It was a long walk, but she enjoyed the activity. With the changing of the seasons, everything had turned to gold with undertones of brown and accents of russet.

Along the way, she inspected the fence with care, knowing her life depended on it. She replaced a couple of rusted wires and found a ditch formed by rainwater. It was deep enough to allow a person to crawl through, so she filled it in with loose rocks and sand before continuing with her circuit.

She'd walked about three-quarters of the way around the property when she found the hole. It was only a few feet from the gate, a gap big enough for a zombie to wriggle through if it wanted. It was hidden from view by a thick bush, the reason nobody had spotted it until now.

The wire was rusted through where it connected to the post. She had to replace each strand by hand and clip off the old. It was a big job, and she resigned herself to spending the rest of the afternoon on the task.

Barely an hour had passed, however, when the rumble of an approaching vehicle put Amy on high alert. Grabbing her shotgun, she hunkered down behind the bush and waited. She didn't have to wait long.

Within seconds, a faded blue truck appeared around the bend, its tires kicking up a cloud of dust. It stopped before the gate, and the passenger door opened with a loud creak. Footsteps approached, crunching on the loose gravel.

Amy's heart was banging in her chest like a drum, and the sour tang of fear coated her tongue. She clutched the gun with sweaty palms, trying to remain calm. To her immense relief, a familiar figure appeared before her eyes.

It was Mrs. Robinson, the next-door-neighbor. Next-door meaning they lived several miles away on a working farm with crops, and horses. They also had a pumpkin patch, and every year, Amy's mom would buy a couple for Halloween. They'd spend the day carving scary faces into the hollowed-out gourds while eating pumpkin pie, Amy's favorite. It was a fond memory that brought a smile to Amy's face.

She straightened up and waved. "Mrs. Robinson. It's me, Amy."

Mrs. Robinson turned to her with a relieved smile. "Amy! I'm so glad to see you. How are you, dear?"

Amy walked over, cradling the shotgun. "I'm okay, Mrs. Robinson."

"I've been so worried. I tried calling your mom a bunch of times, but there's no reception. Ted and I wanted to make a turn before now, but with all the crazy things happening, we haven't had a chance until now."

Mr. Robinson stepped out of the truck and tipped his hat. "Good day, Amy. Is your father here?"

A knot formed in Amy's throat, and she shook her head. "He's not here. He's gone."

"Gone?" Mr. Robinson asked. "What do you mean?"

"He went to town a week ago, and he never came back," Amy said, hot tears burning her eyelids. "I think something happened to him."

Mrs. Robinson gasped. "Oh, I'm so sorry to hear that. What about your mother? Is she home?"

Amy shook her head, the tears spilling over. "She got bitten a few days ago. I buried her in the backyard underneath the lemon tree."

Mrs. Robinson paled, one hand fluttering at the base of her throat. "You're all alone? Oh, my dear. We can't have that, can we Ted?"

Mr. Robinson regarded Amy with a sympathetic look. "Certainly not. It's not safe."

Mrs. Robinson nodded. "You must come with us, dear. We'll take care of you."

Amy stared at the couple, tears still streaming down her face. They were good people. Honest, hardworking, and God-fearing. Her kind of people. While they'd never been house

93

friends, they were a known quantity. Familiar. She longed to take them up on their offer. It would be a relief not to be alone anymore. Alone and scared. They'd look after her like she was their own, that she knew for sure.

"Amy?" Mrs. Robinson said when the silence stretched on too long. "You can trust us, my dear. We won't hurt you."

"I know that Mrs, Robinson, and thank you," Amy said, brushing the tears away. "But I can't."

"Why not?" Mr. Robinson asked with a frown. "You'll be safe with us."

"I'm waiting for my brother. He's on his way," Amy said.

"How long has it been since you heard from him?" Mr. Robinson asked.

"A few days, that's all," Amy said, her tone defiant as if she dared him to disagree.

"Why not leave him a message? That way he'll know where to find you when he gets here," Mr. Robinson answered in a neutral voice.

"But…what about the chickens? The house? I can't just leave it all behind," Amy protested, realizing she was clutching at straws.

"Of course, you can. Take what you want and lock up the rest. The house will be fine, I promise," Mr. Robinson said with an expression of infinite patience on his weathered face.

"I don't know." Amy's mind was in a whirl, twisting one way then the next like a weather vane in a stiff breeze.

"You can bring the chickens too, my dear. We've got space at our farm," Mrs. Robinson said, wringing her hands together.

Amy hesitated. She desperately wanted to accept, but something stopped her. What if Alex never got the message? She'd never see him again, and he was all she had left — the last of her family.

"I'm sorry, Mr. and Mrs. Robinson. I appreciate the offer, but I'd like to wait a few more days. If Alex still hasn't shown up by then, I'll go with you," Amy said.

Mr. Robinson regarded her for a moment before nodding. "Alright. I'll swing by in a week with the truck. If he hasn't come back, we'll load your stuff. Deal?"

"Deal," Amy answered, relieved that he wasn't trying to force her into anything yet. She knew he thought her brother was dead, but she couldn't accept that fact. Not yet. *He's still alive. I know it.*

"Ted! We can't leave her here like this," Mrs. Robinson protested.

"She's old enough to make her own decisions, May," Ted replied. "Besides, she's done well enough on her own so far. A few more days won't make a difference."

Mrs. Robinson chewed on her bottom lip. "Won't you change your mind, Amy? I hate the thought of you being here all alone. What if those things come here?"

"I'll be okay, Mrs. Robinson. It's only a week, and I've got this," Amy said, indicating the shotgun. She didn't mention that she'd already killed her first zombie. Mr. Robinson might change his mind if he heard that little bit of information.

"We'll leave you to it then," Mr. Robinson said, ushering his wife back to the truck. "Lie low, and stay hidden, okay? And keep away from town. Louisville is a madhouse. If anything happens, anything at all, you come to us."

"Will do, Mr. Robinson," Amy replied, watching with sad eyes as the couple departed, the truck rumbling back the way it came.

Once the dust settled, she resumed fixing the hole in the

fence. The entire time, she couldn't help but wonder if she hadn't made the biggest mistake of her life. But her mind was made up. *It's only been four days. I have to give him longer than that.*

She'd stay one more week, waiting for Alex. It had to be enough. Besides, it would grant her the chance to say goodbye to everything she'd ever known. Her home. Her parents. Her childhood.

***

Amy stared at the plate of food in front of her, picking at it without enthusiasm. She wasn't hungry. All day long, she kept wondering if she'd made a mistake turning away the Robinson couple. After they left, she'd completed her chores and kept busy until nightfall. Now she had nothing left to occupy her thoughts, and they were torturing her.

Should she have gone?

Shouldn't she have gone?

What would her mom or dad have said? She wished she knew, wished they were still there with her, beside her. Wished they weren't dead.

Amy ground her teeth in frustration. "If wishes were fishes."

Finally, she wrapped her food and put it in the fridge, determined to get some sleep. She was tired, after all. The past few nights had not been kind to her. She was about to walk up the stairs when a noise caused her to pause. It was the sound of an engine, and she quickly grabbed the shotgun.

With shaking hands, she unlocked the front door and peered outside. A faint light shone up the driveway, and she guessed whoever it was had parked in front of the locked gate. Who could it be? The Robinson's? Alex? Strangers?

Hope rose in Amy's chest, tempered by caution. Maybe it

was Alex, and maybe it wasn't. She tucked the gate keys into her pocket just in case.

Stepping lightly, she ran down the porch to get a closer look, taking care not to reveal her presence. When she had a good view of the gate, she paused. It was a bike, and nobody she knew of rode a motorcycle. Unless...

Again hope rose at the thought that it might be Alex, and she carefully moved closer. Pausing a few feet away, she raised the shotgun and aimed it at the rider sitting on the back of the bike.

In a loud voice, she shouted out a challenge, trying to sound calm and confident. Not at all like the blubbery mess she was on the inside. "Who's there? This is private property, and strangers aren't welcome."

"Amy? It's me, Alex," shouted a familiar voice. *His* voice.

Amy lowered the gun, almost too scared to believe it was true. "Alex? Is that really you?"

"It's me, and I need help. I'm hurt," he said in response to her frantic queries.

"Hurt? Oh, no!" Amy cried. "Hold on. I'm coming."

She rushed forward and undid the padlock before swinging the gate open. Alex rode through, his figure hunched low over the tank. Amy checked the road behind him, looking for zombies, but it was clean. One less thing to worry about, at least.

After locking the gates once more, she ran back to the house. Panic blossomed in her chest along the way. She'd never seen Alex hurt before. He never even got a cold. Not so much as a sniffle. What if it was serious? What if he died?

For a moment, she almost allowed fear to overwhelm her. Then she spotted him lying on the ground. Amy shook her head, determination washing away her uncertainty. Her brother was hurt, and he needed her help. She had to be strong. "I won't let anything happen to him. He's home now, and that's all that matters."

Chapter 15 - Alex

Alex rode through the gate with the last bit of strength he possessed. He came to a stop in front of the house, his house, and promptly keeled over. His legs couldn't hold him upright any longer, and the bike weighed a ton.

After spending a freezing night in a dilapidated old shack, cold, hungry, and in pain, he'd tackled the final leg home. After several hours of sheer torture, he'd made it, and now he had nothing left to give.

His hearing was dim, and he only vaguely became aware of Amy's voice, urging him to get up. Somehow, despite her petite frame, she dragged the bike off his pinned leg and hoisted him up.

He clung to her, willing his legs to work. Together, they staggered up the porch steps and into the house where he collapsed onto the nearest couch. That was when it all went black.

Alex woke the next morning to find himself tucked into a cocoon of blankets. His boots were gone, and his wound had been dressed with fresh bandages. A glass of water stood waiting on the side table along with a couple of painkillers, and he swallowed them greedily.

On the couch opposite him, Amy lay curled into a little ball.

99

Her blonde hair spilled around her face in a golden waterfall. The sight made him smile. She always slept like that, rolled up with her knees tucked beneath her chin. It made him realize how much he'd missed her. How much he'd missed all of them, and now his parents were gone. She was all he had left in the world.

He must have made a sound because Amy's eyes fluttered open and fixed on his face with alarm. She jolted upright. "Are you okay? Are you in pain? Can I get you anything?"

Alex shook his head. "I'm fine."

He wasn't though. Not by a long shot. Despite his best efforts, the wound in his side had festered. A raging fever had hold of his limbs, and he alternated between sweating like a pig and shivering until his teeth chattered.

She jumped off the couch and pressed a cool hand to his forehead. "You're sick."

It was a statement, not a question, and he couldn't deny it even though he wanted to spare her the worry. "Yes."

"I cleaned your wound, but it's gone bad. You need antibiotics," Amy added.

"Which we don't have."

"No," she replied with a shake of her head. "I checked mom's cupboards and the first-aid kit, but there's nothing. We have to get you to a doctor."

"There aren't any doctors available. Not now. No hospital either," Alex said, tugging at his collar as his skin overheated. He threw off the covers he'd slept under as sweat burst from his pores. Within seconds, he was soaked to the bone as the fever raged through his body.

Once the bout passed, Amy pressed another glass of water into his hands along with a bowl of soup. "Eat. You need to keep your strength up."

"Thanks," he mumbled through spoonfuls of the beefy broth, relishing the noodles and bits of carrot that floated around in the thick concoction. It eased away the hollow feeling in his stomach, and he felt much better once he got it all down.

While he ate, Amy paced up and down in the living room, her heart-shaped face scrunched up into a frown. "There has to be something. Someone who can help."

"There's no one, Amy. It's every man for himself now, trust me," he replied, shifting on the couch with a grimace of pain. "It's chaos out there. How do you think I got this stab wound?"

She rounded on him in a fury. "Don't you dare give up on me, Alex. You didn't come all this way to die on me. I'm not burying any more family. Not today, and not tomorrow."

Alex winced. "I'm sorry you had to do that, Amy. I'm sorry I wasn't here for you when you needed me."

"That's okay. The fact is, you're here now, and that's all that matters. What happened to you, anyway? What's it like out there?"

Alex filled her in on everything that he'd experienced and seen since the outbreak began. He took care not to gloss over any of the facts. She needed to know what was out there. Half-truths wouldn't save her from the worst while preparedness might.

Amy listened the entire time, not interrupting once. When he was finished, she resumed her furious pacing before coming to an abrupt halt. "I've got it. I'll take you to the Robinson's."

"Huh?" Alex asked. "Who's that?"

"Our neighbors. Don't you remember them?" she asked.

"Vaguely. When last did you see them?"

In brief terms, Amy told him about her encounter with the

couple and their offer. "I'm sure they'll be able to help you."

Alex thought it over. "Well, it's worth a shot."

Amy nodded. "Let me grab a few things. You stay right there."

Alex snorted. "As if I've got anywhere to go, but can't I take a shower, at least? I stink."

"You do," Amy agreed. "But you'd better hurry up. The sooner we get your medicine, the happier I'll be."

"Yes, ma'am," Alex replied, amused by this bossy side of her. She'd certainly grown into a feisty young woman while he was gone.

He dragged his aching body up the stairs for a quick shower and fresh clothes. It was worth the pain to be clean again and dressed in something that didn't reek of sweat. In the meantime, Amy packed a basket of food and water, pulled their mom's old car out of the garage, and carried his saddlebags inside.

"You've got a lot of guns here," she remarked.

"Yup, and we'll need every single one in the days to come," he remarked. "Is there any ammo in the safe?"

"I think so," Amy replied, bustling off to check. She returned with a couple of boxes, and they reloaded all the weapons.

Amy wore her mom's pistol on her belt, and carried the shotgun, while Alex stuck to his carbine, sidearm, and knife. The hammer and other pistol they tucked into the glove compartment in the car, while Amy got the extra knife.

She stared at it with distaste. "This is the same knife that guy stuck into you."

"Maybe, but it's a good quality blade," Alex replied, watching as she added the sheath to her belt. "It'll come in handy, trust me."

"If you say so," she replied. "Now let's get going. It's after six in the morning already."

"What about the chickens?" he asked.

"I let them out and scattered some feed," Amy said. "Even if we don't come back they'll be fine. They can live off worms and insects."

"Good to know," he replied, walking to the driver's side with a decided limp. He felt better after eating and washing, but he was still a far way from anything resembling his old self.

Amy shook her head. "You can't drive. Not like that."

"I can, and I will, Missy. I'll be damned if I let my kid sister chauffeur me around like an invalid," Alex said. "Besides, it's not that far."

Amy sighed. "Fine, but if you crash mom's car, she's coming back to haunt you."

Alex laughed for the first time in days, the permanent knot of ice in his belly fading away. Even under the circumstances, it felt good to be home.

Chapter 16 - Dylan

Dylan drove for about ten minutes before she pulled over to check the suitcase she'd loaded into the back. A glance at the mirror convinced her of the necessity. Vandalia was only a few minutes away, and from what Maddie had told her, there could be roadblocks and militia roaming about.

There was no chance in hell that any sane person would allow her into their town looking the way she did. Blood had dried in runnels across her face, and her hair and clothes were matted with the stuff. The flannel sleeve bandage had done its job but looked ridiculous. She had to make an effort to clean up before she went ahead. Much as she hated the idea of braving the town and its possibly hostile inhabitants, she had no choice. There was no way around it that she knew off, and she couldn't risk getting lost.

She unzipped the bag on the back seat and rummaged through the contents. It contained a change of clothes, a bag of toiletries, a book of poetry, a dead cellphone, and a towel. "Is that it? No food, no weapons, nothing?"

Dylan slammed the bag down as a fit of rage overtook her. Everything that had happened to her since she'd first left her apartment the day before came rushing back. The mad rush at the store, the zombies, getting bitten, Ben abandoning her,

Frankie, the map, everything.

"Why me, huh? Why is it always me?" she screamed in frustration at no one and everyone. "Haven't I been through enough?"

Maddie's face flashed before her eyes. Cold and self-righteous. The words she'd uttered rang through Dylan's ears. Full of hatred and spite. *"The fact remains, you're a monster, and you deserve to die."*

"Oh, yeah? Wait until I catch you, you smug little bitch. Even Kyle won't save you then. I'll rip you apart with my bare hands and feast on your beating heart." A red tint washed the world in blood, and Dylan lost herself in a sea of anger. Her body moved of its own volition as she raged at her surroundings, not caring who or what might hear her.

At the back of her mind, she was aware of the loss of control but couldn't stop herself. When she finally came to, her throat was raw from all the screaming, and she'd beaten her fists black and blue against the roof of the car.

Exhausted, she sagged backward and closed her eyes until the dizziness passed. Her hands ached, and so did her head. Even worse, she couldn't understand why she'd lost it like that. Sure, she hated Maddie, and if she ran into the woman, it wouldn't be pretty, but... "This isn't me. Why am I acting like this?"

Dylan had no answers to any of her questions and dragged her attention back to the present. "Let's get cleaned up and get through Vandalia. After that...well...we'll see."

She pulled the suitcase over again and rummaged through the clothes, removing a fresh button-down shirt and sleeveless vest. The owner had been a man, but a slender one luckily. With her bloodied top and jacket changed, she felt better already. It still didn't solve her other problems, though.

105

With a copious amount of spit, she cleaned the worst of the blood from her face with the towel. The matted hairdo was a complete loss, however. Even touching the injured area was a no-go. In the end, she settled for a bandana fashioned from a t-shirt she found in the bag, folding and tying it back in the nape of her neck. "Ah, crap. I look like shit, but it'll have to do, I guess."

The bandage on her arm had to stay put. She had nothing to replace it with, nor was there anything to eat or drink in the car. To top it off, she had a fever. Her forehead radiated heat. After swallowing another couple of painkillers, she climbed back behind the wheel and mentally prepared herself for what lay ahead. "Keep it together, Dylan. Fort Knox isn't that far. You can still make it."

First, she had to get through Vandalia and drove toward it with a sense of trepidation. A board announced that the town lay straight ahead, and her eyes soon picked it up against the horizon. As she neared the entrance, a roadblock loomed, and Dylan slowed to a stop in front of it. She opened her window and stuck her head out, evaluating the scene.

The barrier was made up of a few parked cars, and she could discern movement behind them. The barrel of a gun pointed at her over the roof of one. Several seconds passed in ominous silence before a voice on loudspeaker announced, "Get out of the vehicle with your hands above your head."

Dylan hesitated, but in reality, she had no choice. Opening the door, she stepped out with her hands held at shoulder-height. The sun shone in her eyes, and she had to squint to look ahead. The warmth felt good on her aching body, though, and for a brief moment, she closed her eyes and imagined she was elsewhere. Standing on a sun-drenched beach in the Bahamas, maybe, with a cocktail in one hand and a cheeseburger in the other. Her stomach cramped in protest, and her dry mouth produced a tiny amount of drool. A feat she'd have thought impossible in her current dehydrated state.

The crunch of boots on the asphalt ruined her fantasy, and she watched a figure approach with wary caution. He stopped a few feet away and eyed her with a curious stare, his hands on his hips. He was young, too young to be in charge of the town but old enough to think he was.

"Are you in charge here?" Dylan asked, not lowering her hands.

"Yes, I am," he said, flashing her a grin that was all teeth and no substance. "Can I help you?"

"I need to pass through," Dylan said.

"Sorry, but I can't allow that. We're on lockdown."

"But, it's the only way," Dylan protested.

The stranger shrugged and tucked his hands into his pockets. "Not my problem."

"You can't be serious. All I need to do is pass through. I won't stop anywhere or take anything, I promise," Dylan said.

"You'll have to take the long way around, I guess..." His eyes flicked between her and her car. "Unless you have something to trade?"

"Are you blackmailing me?" Dylan asked with narrowed eyes.

"I wouldn't call it that. Think of it as a toll fee," the stranger said.

"Well, I haven't got anything to give, so you can forget about it. No food, or water," Dylan said.

"You've got a gun," he said, pointing at her pistol.

Dylan shook her head. "Forget it. No trade."

The stranger laughed. "Alright. How about a different kind

of trade then?"

A cold shiver ran down Dylan's spine when she noticed the way his eyes raked her body from top to bottom. "Woah, eyes up here. I'm not a slab of meat, you know?"

"That's funny because that's exactly what you are. Your body is just another commodity on the market. Lucky for you, it's worth something, even banged up as you are." The stranger rocked back on his heels, his hands still in his pockets, and his disregard infuriated Dylan.

"Seriously? You want me to sleep with you for passage through your shitty little town?" Dylan said, hot blood flushing her cheeks. A flame of anger churned in her gut, twisting, and turning.

"When you put it like that, it does sound rather bad. How about I throw in some supplies as payment? Maybe even a can of fuel? I'm sure you'll make it worth my while," he said with a grin.

The flame curling inside Dylan's stomach exploded into full-blown rage. It burned through her veins until she thought she would combust and go supernova on him. Her hands twitched, and she had to fight the urge to strangle him on the spot. A vivid picture of his bulging eyes beneath her squeezing fingers caused her to smile.

"What are you smiling at?" the stranger asked, removing his hands from his pockets. He took a step back, clearly unnerved by her bared teeth.

Dylan didn't answer. Instead, her eyes roved over the barricade behind him, spotting two more guns leveled at her. That brought the total up to three. She was outmanned and outgunned, but there was no chance in hell that she'd trade her body. A wave of recklessness washed over her, and she laughed. *Might as well go out in a blaze of glory.*

She took a sudden step to the side, placing her behind the open door of her car. At the same time, she hunkered down, whipped out her gun, and pointed it at the stranger's face through the open window. "I'm smiling because, in the next ten seconds, I'm going to blow a hole right through that stupid grin of yours."

The stranger froze, the cocky smile vanishing from his face as he stared down the cold length of her gun barrel. "Don't be an idiot. We've got guns on you. You'll be dead the second you pull that trigger."

"Maybe, but I'd rather go out like that than let you touch even one hair on my head," she said. "Now, call off your men, or I'll kill you right where you stand. Got it?"

He raised his hands and waved at the men behind him. "Back off, guys. This bitch is crazy. She'll kill me for sure."

Dylan smirked. "You've got that right, at least. It seems you're not completely dumb."

He shot her a venomous look. "Now what?"

"Now, I'm going to get in my car, and you're going to join me. Your buddies there will allow me to drive through your town, unharmed, or I'll shoot you. Got that?"

The stranger swallowed. "You'll never make it."

"Maybe not, but if I go, I'm taking you with me. We can be buddies on the bus ride to hell," Dylan said. It was a crazy plan and doomed to failure, but she was out of options. She had to get through the town or risk not making it to Fort Knox at all.

Before she could put her plan into motion, however, a ripple of movement ran through the assembled people behind the barricade. The loudspeaker came on again, and Dylan frowned at the message, unsure what to do next.

"Hello, miss. It's Dr. Hayes here. I'm the resident surgeon, and I'm coming out to talk to you. I'm unarmed. Please, don't shoot me."

Dylan hesitated as a tall, slender man walked out into the road with his hands raised. She glanced at her hostage. "Maybe this is your lucky day. Maybe not."

She raised her voice and shouted back. "Alright, Dr. Hayes. I'll bite, but keep your hands where I can see them. If anyone makes a move, I'll pump this boy so full of holes there won't be enough left of him to bury."

The stranger glared at her. "Boy? Who's your boy? My name is Ray."

"Shut up, Ray," Dylan said as Dr. Hayes acknowledged her challenge.

"Understood. I'm coming out," the doctor said, slowly walking toward her.

Dylan looked at Ray. "Let's hope Dr. Hayes has more sense than you do, you little shit. Accosting a defenseless woman like that. You should be ashamed of yourself."

Ray's face reddened. "Whatever."

"Remember. I'm holding the gun, so don't try anything stupid," Dylan said before turning back to the approaching doctor. Maybe, just maybe, she could talk her way out of the mess she found herself in even though the odds were stacked against her. Either way, she'd soon find out.

Chapter 17 - Dylan

Doctor Hayes paused a few feet away from Dylan and stared at her with keen blue eyes from underneath a mop of dark brown hair. She judged him to be in his early thirties, and he moved with the kind of casual ease that spoke of confidence. Not lowering his hands, he tipped his head forward. "Good morning, Miss…"

"You can call me Dylan," she said, keeping the gun steady.

"Alright, Dylan. I'm here to negotiate for the release of young Ray over there. His father is very anxious to have him returned unharmed," Doctor Hayes said, nodding at a distant figure over his shoulder.

"Well, you can tell his father that he should teach his children some manners," Dylan said, shooting Ray a poisonous glare.

"I take it the boy said something he shouldn't have?" Doctor Hayes asked.

"I'm not a boy!" Ray protested, his face flushing with angry blood. "What is it with you people?"

"What he did say to you?" Doctor Hayes asked, ignoring Ray completely.

"First, he refused me passage through your town. Then he suggested a trade. My body being part of the goods, of course," Dylan answered.

Doctor Hayes shook his head. "I'm sorry, miss. That's an awful thing to suggest to a lady and against our town policy."

"Just Dylan, please. I'm nobody's miss."

"Fair enough. How about you call me Ethan? I prefer it to Doctor Hayes."

"Fine, Ethan, but tell me something. If Ray's actions are against town policy, how come they sent him out to talk to me and not somebody else?" Dylan asked.

"We're shorthanded at the moment. Patrolling a town this size is quite a task," Ethan answered, his voice mild. "When you arrived, Ray and his friends were the only ones manning the roadblock. They sent for Ray's father and me, but we've just arrived."

Dylan mulled this over, wondering if she could trust Ethan. Her instincts were telling her she could, but it was a tough call. "So, what happens now?"

"You and I negotiate your terms while Ray returns to his father unharmed," Ethan said. "I can replace him as a hostage if need be."

Dylan chewed on her bottom lip before nodding. "Deal. You'd make a better hostage anyway. I'm guessing with his attitude, not many people would miss him if he dies."

A faint smile graced Ethan's lips. "Probably not, whereas I'm the only town surgeon."

Ray sputtered at their words, his face rapidly turning the shade of boiled beetroot. "You can't be serious. Nobody would care? I'm right here, you know."

Dylan raised an eyebrow. "You're assuming I care what you think."

Ray snarled, unable to contain himself. "Bitch."

Before Dylan could reply, Ethan turned on Ray. "Go back

to your father before you kill us both, and next time, leave the negotiations up to the grownups."

Ray stomped back to the roadblock, muttering evil phrases every step of the way. Dylan watched him go with a worried frown. "He'll do something stupid one of these days."

"Not if I have anything to say about it," Ethan said, turning back to her. "You're injured. Let me help you."

"You want to help me?" Dylan asked with a disbelieving laugh. "That'd be a first."

"I take it you've had a rough couple of days?" Ethan asked.

"A rough couple of years about sums it up," Dylan said, rising slowly to her feet. Her calves cramped in protest, and she leaned on the doorframe to stay upright.

"That's too bad, but if you let me, I'll patch you up. It looks like you need it."

Dylan shrugged. "I'm okay. What about passage through your town?"

"Granted."

"That easily? What about him?" Dylan asked, pointing at Ray's retreating figure.

"Forget about him. Ever since the outbreak, he and a few like him have taken to thinking they're big chiefs around here, but they don't run the show."

"Who does?"

"The Mayor and his council of which I am a part of," Ethan said.

"I see." Dylan hesitated. "Do you know a woman called Maddie?"

Ethan shook his head. "Doesn't ring a bell."

"She was on her way here with her son, Kyle. Her mother lives in Vandalia. She'd have arrived sometime yesterday afternoon."

"Could be, but I was at the clinic all day. If she did show up, she'd have been escorted to her mother's house by one of the guards," David said. "Is she a friend of yours?"

"Not exactly. I'm just curious, that's all," Dylan said, deciding not to tell him more for the moment. Who knew how much influence either Maddie or her mother had among the townspeople. It'd be better to steer clear of the crazed woman altogether, much though she'd have liked to see justice done.

A sudden wave of dizziness crashed over her, and she sagged against the doorframe. Ethan noticed and took a step closer. "You're dead on your feet. Let me help you, please. I promise you'll come to no harm."

"You swear it?"

"I do."

Too tired to argue further, Dylan gave in. "Alright, but no funny business. Once you've patched me up, I'll be on my way. No questions asked."

"Deal," Ethan said, taking another tentative step forward. "Let me drive. That way, you can keep an eye on me at all times if it makes you feel any better."

Dylan climbed into the car and slid over to the passenger side, making sure to keep her gun at the ready. "She's all yours."

With careful movements, Ethan followed, sliding behind the wheel and starting the engine. Before he drove off, he wrinkled his nose. "It smells like death in here."

Dylan managed a laugh. "Death and zombies."

"Something tells me there's a story behind that," he said.

"You could say so," Dylan said, shifting around in her seat to get comfortable. "Maybe, I'll even tell you one day."

They approached the roadblock, and Ethan waved at the

guards to let them through. A furious Ray stared at them before blasting off a volley of words at an older man, presumably his father, who stood next to him.

"Is that his dad?" Dylan asked, eyeing the square-shouldered, white-haired man with caution.

"That's right. Let me talk to him for a second," Ethan said.

"No! You can't leave me here alone," Dylan protested, acutely aware of the hostile looks being directed at her from all direction.

Ethan turned to her and placed one calming hand on her shoulder. "Dylan, please trust me. I won't let anyone hurt you, but I have to diffuse the situation before it gets any worse."

Something in Ethan's gaze caused Dylan to pause in mid-panic, and her fluttering heart slowed to a steady beat. "You'll look out for me? For real?"

Ethan nodded. "I've got you. I promise."

Dylan sucked in a deep breath. "Alright."

She watched with more than just a tinge of fear as he got out of the car, leaving her alone and exposed. He pulled Ray's father off to the side, and they talked. It was an intense conversation with Ray interfering more than once. At last, after a sharp command from his dad, the boy skulked off to a corner. He was joined by two more guys, and the trio kept looking at Dylan in a manner that made her want to squirm in her seat.

Instead, she flashed Ray the middle-finger and kept an eye on them in the mirror with her gun in her lap. She had only four bullets left, but one of them would find a home in Ray's skull if he so much as twitched in her direction. Finally, Ethan returned, his expression taut.

"How did it go?" she asked.

"He's not happy with you pulling a gun on Ray, but I told

him what the little prick said to you, so he gets it," Ethan said. "Kind of."

"What do you mean, kind of?"

"Forget about it. He won't bother you. That's the main thing."

Dylan wasn't a hundred percent happy with his explanation, but she decided to let it go. "Fine. Where to next?"

"I'm taking you to my practice to treat your wounds. After that, you're free to leave anytime you want. I'll even escort you out. Sound good?" Ethan asked.

"I guess so. It's not like I have much of a choice," Dylan answered.

The doctor drove off, and after a while, she tried to relax. The timer on her wrist was running down, each precious second another moment lost. Still, she wouldn't get far injured as she was, and who knew what lay ahead. She had to be ready for anything — fighting fit.

When they reached his practice, she eyed the empty parking lot and lonesome sign with a dubious frown. "No sick townspeople today?"

"There are bound to be, but they'll all be at the local clinic. I've been spending most of my time there since this all began," Ethan said.

"Why?"

"There are two assistant nurses, a veterinarian, and a few volunteers to help. We decided to pool our resources since the outbreak began," he said.

"Smart. Was it your idea?" Dylan said.

He laughed. "It was. We needed a central place where people could get treated quickly, and that was it."

"Like I said. Smart."

With a grunt of pain, Dylan levered her aching body out of

the car and followed Ethan up the steps to the front door. He unlocked and led her through the empty waiting room, pausing only to switch on the lights.

He turned to her with an appraising look, taking in her bloodied clothes and matted hair. "Would you like to take a shower? I have a full bathroom in the back that you can use. I might even be able to scrounge up some fresh clothes for you."

"Clothes?"

"You'd be surprised what the receptionists have left behind over the years."

Dylan hesitated and glanced at the watch on her wrist, but the thought of a hot shower was impossible to resist. "I'd love to. Thanks."

She waited while he rummaged around in a closet at the back. With a yell of triumph, he produced a t-shirt and a jersey which looked close to her size. He rounded it off with a pair of socks and a scarf. "Here you go. I'll make some coffee while you wash up. There are soap and towels inside the bathroom. Enjoy."

Dylan's ears perked up at the mention of coffee, and her parched mouth suddenly reminded her how thirsty she was. Rushing inside, she opened the cold-water tap on the basin and gulped down as much water as her shrunken stomach could hold. The cold liquid revived her senses, and some of the light-headedness faded away. "Oh, that feels so much better."

With care, she placed her gun on a small stool and locked the door. As much as she liked the doctor, she still didn't fully trust him. Unwinding the cloth tied around her head took some doing, matted as it was with dried blood.

After another long drink of water, she opened the shower taps until steam rose from the tiles and misted the mirrors. A floral body wash and shampoo waited on a shelf, and she scooped them up with a grin. As the air grew pleasantly warm, she eyed the waiting shower with drooping eyelids. "I am so going to enjoy this."

Chapter 18 - Dylan

She stripped off her clothes and stepped into the stream of hot water, groaning with pleasure when it hit her skin. With careful fingers, she washed the blood from her hair, working the shampoo into the matted locks until the water ran red. She didn't stop there, soaping every inch of her body as she went. Old bandages and band-aids fell to her feet, and she tossed them into the waiting bin.

Finally, she dared to take a look at her naked body in the tall mirror on the opposite wall and sucked in a horrified breath. The bite on her arm was beginning to rot, and the black veins had spread up to her shoulder. Tendrils crept along her back and chest, a road map of infection.

Her eyes were shadowed, her cheeks hollow and pale. Bruises and abrasions covered her arms and legs. The worst was the spot where Frankie's undead boyfriend had tried to take a chunk from her arm. The area was a hideous mottled purple. She looked like death and felt like it too.

"I'm already half-zombie, I guess," she said with a muted laugh. It wasn't funny, though, seeing herself rot from within. Anything but funny.

Averting her gaze from the mirror, she continued to wash as well as she could, rinsing all the dried blood and puss from the bite wound until the water ran clear. Afterward, she dried off and wrapped her hair in a clean towel before getting dressed. Frankie's boots and jeans would have to do, but at least she had fresh socks to wear. The new shirt and jersey was an improvement too, the material soft and warm against her skin.

By this point, she was almost too tired to move, but there could be no rest for her. Not when the clock continued its relentless countdown. With her gun once more at her side, she made her way to Ethan's examination room.

He was waiting for her with a hot cup of coffee just like he'd promised. Even better, there was a whole plate of chocolate chip cookies too. Nursing the warm porcelain cup between her palms, she savored the strong brew one sip at a time while munching on the cookies. Gradually, the cramp in her stomach eased as she filled up on food and caffeine. "Thank you. I can't remember when last I've eaten."

"That's okay. I took the liberty of packing you some food and water for the road too, and I topped up your gas tank," Ethan said with a smile that reached his eyes. A genuine smile.

Surprised, Dylan stared at him. "You did? Why?"

"Why not? I'm a doctor. It's my job to look after people, and you need it," Ethan replied.

"Yeah, but still. It's every man for himself nowadays," Dylan said. "Actually, scratch that. It's always been every man for himself."

He regarded her with somber eyes. "You've had a tough life, haven't you?"

Dylan shrugged. "I guess so. It doesn't help to whine about it, though."

"No, but you can talk to me if you want to," he said.

"Thanks for the offer, but the past is best left in the past."

"And now, what are your plans for the future?" he asked.

Dylan hesitated before deciding to come clean. "If I even have a future."

"What do you mean?"

Rolling back her sleeve, she showed him the bite mark on her arm. "I'm living on borrowed time, doctor."

He stared at the wound with a strange mixture of loss and sadness. "I'm sorry."

"Why are you sorry? It's not your fault."

"Because losing you would be a tragedy for this world. You're an extraordinary woman, Dylan."

She laughed disbelievingly. "Yeah? You think so?"

He nodded, not smiling back. "I know so. You're strong. A fighter."

His words evoked warmth in her chest that she hadn't felt in ages. Attraction. Not that she could afford any complications. Shrugging it off, she said, "Anyway, it's why I need passage. There's a cure at Fort Knox, but I have to get there before I turn. Once I die, it's game over."

"I see. Do you have enough time?" he asked, leaning forward.

"Just under two days. I can make it if nothing else goes wrong," she said with a quick glance at her watch.

"I can't believe it. A cure." Ethan jumped up. "We'd better hurry then. Can't have you missing your deadline, can we?"

Dylan placed her empty cup on his desk. "Indeed not."

He made her sit on the bed while he gathered a few supplies from the closet. She swung her legs back and forth, feeling relaxed after the hot bath. She yawned. "Do you have anything to keep me awake? I'm dead tired."

Ethan shook his head. "I'll give you a shot of vitamins to boost your immune system and another of antibiotics, but what you really need is rest."

"The one thing I don't have time for."

He shot her a distressed look but remained silent. After snapping on a set of gloves, he said, "Let's see what we're dealing with."

Dylan nodded and began pointing out her various aches and pains. Most of it was bruising with a few abrasions that needed disinfecting, but the cut on her hand required more care.

"It's too late for stitches, I'm afraid, but I've wrapped it up as best as I can," Ethan said, securing a bandage firmly in place with tape. "Can you tell me what happened to you? It must be quite a story."

"I suppose." Dylan told him about her trip to the supermarket, getting bitten, leaving town, finding Frankie, and even Maddie and Kyle. It took her mind off the pain while he worked.

"They burned people alive?" he asked, shocked by that part of her story. "I knew things were going to hell, but that's murder!"

"I know. It's crazy out there. They'd burn me too if they could. So would Maddie," Dylan said.

Ethan shook his head as he examined the cut on her head. "She tried to kill you, that's for sure. That is one nasty wound. You're lucky she didn't fracture your skull."

"I wouldn't call it luck." Dylan went on to tell him about Kyle saving her and spending the night with a dead zombie in the car.

"No wonder it smells like death in there. Should I add a can of air freshener to your supplies?" Ethan asked with a grin.

Dylan laughed, appreciating his attempt at levity as he injected the area around the gash. "Anything but roses, please."

He arched an eyebrow. "Not a fan?"

"Nope, I'm an amber and musk kind of girl." She gasped as

122

the anesthetic burned away all feeling until her eyes watered. "Holy crap, that hurts."

"This will only take a minute." With smooth efficiency, he disinfected her scalp and stitched up the wound. Afterward, he cleaned the other, smaller cut that Frankie's boyfriend had given her before stepping back. "Right. I put four stitches in there. Have someone take a look at it as soon as you reach Fort Knox, and for God's sake, try not to get injured again."

"I can't make any promises," Dylan said with a rueful smile. "Trouble seems to find me."

"Yes, that's what worries me," Ethan said, as he slid back the sleeve on her arm. "Now, let's take a look at this zombie bite of yours."

Dylan swallowed when she caught a whiff of rotting flesh and quickly looked away. "It's bad, isn't it?"

"The flesh around the edges is decomposing, and the infection seems quite advanced. I'd say you're almost at the halfway point now," Ethan said in somber tones as he swabbed the area with alcohol before wrapping it up.

Dylan looked at the timer on her wrist. "Sounds about right. I've got about forty-five hours left."

He injected her with a cocktail of antibiotics and handed over a bottle of pills with strict instructions. "Here, take these. It will help to control the fever. You're burning up. There's not much more I can do for you, though. I wish there were."

Dylan stared at the pills before meeting his gaze. "You've done more than enough, thank you."

A long moment of silence passed as they stared into each other's eyes. Dylan was the first to look away, uncomfortable with the energy flowing between them. She couldn't afford to care. Not now. Like this.

123

"I've got to go," she whispered.

"I know. I'll drive," he answered.

As they walked outside, Dylan couldn't help but reflect on the unfortunate timing of their meeting. If only it had been before the outbreak. Things might have been so different then. But it wasn't, and she was running out of time.

Tick, tock.

Tick, tock.

Chapter 19 - Dylan

Ethan drove her through town, and she couldn't help but notice the ongoing activity. Houses were being torn down, and the material was driven away while people rushed along the sidewalks with hunched shoulders. Others queued at shops for groceries doled out in brown paper bags.

Trucks with armed men policed the street, and they were stopped more than once and questioned. Luckily, Ethan was well-known and held in high esteem, so they got no trouble.

"It's like a concentration camp," Dylan said after a while.

"Really?" Ethan asked. "Why do you say that? We're securing the town against zombie attacks."

"Maybe, but I've seen how quickly things can go wrong. Ray is your first example. He's driving around with a gun and feeling important. He's the man, in charge of the safety of other citizens. Soon, he starts feeling like they owe him, while outsiders are nothing but trash. In no time at all, girls are forced to give it up to Ray and his cronies while the best supplies go to feed and house them."

"That's just Ray. Maybe one or two others. The rest of us aren't like that," Ethan protested. "We just want to keep people safe, fed, and healthy."

"I know. You're a good guy, but how long will it take before you're outvoted? Ray's dad wasn't thrilled with my actions despite having good cause. That means he leans toward his son's ideals. Hell, he probably taught them to Ray. And Maddie. How long do you think it'll take before her dogma spreads through the rest of the town?"

Ethan was silent for a long time after she spoke. Finally, he said, "I hope you're wrong. I grew up in this town. I'm their doctor. I've nursed these people through sickness and health, caught countless babies, seen others pass away. Your vision of the future is a nightmare."

"For your sake, I hope I'm wrong. But I just drove through a town who burned an innocent girl on the stake. These are terrible times, Ethan. And people are capable of terrible things."

"I guess you're right. I'll have to make sure it doesn't come to that," Ethan said.

"I hope you succeed." Dylan stared ahead as they neared another roadblock. "Is this it?"

"Yup. This is where we part ways," Ethan said. He stopped in front of the barrier and spoke to the guards, telling them to let her pass.

The guards seemed kind enough and even greeted her while Ray and his friends were nowhere to be seen. A decided relief. "Thank you for everything, Ethan."

"It was my pleasure, Dylan. Your supplies are in the trunk, and you've got a full tank of gas. I hope you make it to Fort Knox on time," Ethan said, gazing at her with his earnest blue eyes.

A few seconds passed in awkward silence as each of them searched for the right thing to say. Secretly, Dylan wished Ethan could've gone with her to Fort Knox, and he didn't look eager to see her go either. But, they each had their road to travel, and it wasn't together. Not now.

"If you ever need to, you'll know where to find me," Dylan said.

"Likewise," Ethan replied, before getting out so she could scoot over. Once settled behind the wheel, the guards opened the barricade, and she had little option but to drive through.

A final wave and then Ethan was gone, retreating to a distant figure in her rearview mirror. The roadblock closed, completely cutting him off from view. Dylan swallowed on a sudden lump in her throat as tears threatened to undo her fragile composure. For the first time, she felt truly alone. Not just alone, but lonely too.

Several miles passed without incident, and she was beginning to grow thirsty again. Hot too. Her fever was growing worse. With the supplies in the trunk, that would mean a quick stop to get water. Before she could pull over, however, a truck appeared on the horizon behind her. It was moving fast, its silhouette growing larger by the second.

Dylan stared at it with narrowed eyes. It could only come from one place. Vandalia. And she could think of only two people who might want to see her again. Ethan and Ray. She strongly doubted it was Ethan racing after her at such breakneck speed. So, it had to be Ray, and he wasn't about to bring her flowers.

"Son of a…" She pulled her gun from its holster and placed it on the seat next to her. "If it's Ray, I'm going to kill him this time."

She cast her eyes around to see if there was anywhere she could take shelter, someplace safe where she could fight Ray off, but there was nothing. Nothing but open fields filled with patches of scraggly brush and trees.

Dylan tried going faster, pushing the car to its limits, but the truck kept getting closer by the minute. It was faster than her. Much faster.

"Running isn't an option, it seems. Neither is hiding. I'll have to fight them off," she muttered as fear stirred in the pit of her stomach. She thought of *them* because she couldn't imagine the sniveling Ray coming after her alone. Nope. He'd bring his buddies with him for back-up.

A minute ticked by as the two vehicles raced across the asphalt. The truck slowly gained while Dylan braced herself for the worst. She was scared, her stomach churning at the thought of what was to come. A fight to the death in which she was outnumbered and outgunned in every way. If she hoped to survive, she'd have to use her wits.

Dylan licked her dry lips as she cast around for a way out, a trick, anything that could save her. All the while, Ray kept gaining until she could make out his face in the mirror. He grinned, sensing her gaze.

Just as she'd thought, he'd brought along two of his buddies as well. The same two who'd stared at her before. That complicated matters. She didn't know what she was going to do. All she did know was that she wouldn't give up. Not a chance. "Come and get it, asshole. I'll make you regret chasing after me. That's a promise."

Chapter 20 - Dylan

Dylan swallowed hard as Ray's truck drew level with her car. Her hands shook on the wheel, and she flexed her fingers to get a better grip. Her gut churned, and she regretted stuffing herself with cookies in Ethan's office earlier. She'd have been better off with an empty stomach.

Ray waved at her to pull over, a wide grin splitting his face from ear to ear. His buddies were laughing too. They were confident they had her. Sure there was no escape, and they were probably right.

Dylan refused to look at them. Instead, she focused on the road, looking for anything that might help her. There was nothing. The highway stretched ahead as straight as an arrow, a smooth gray snake that cut through the landscape. On either side, spread a barren world. It was as if they'd fallen off the face of the earth. There wasn't a single farmhouse to offer hope. No one to help. No other cars. And the nearest town too far to be of any assistance. She was on her own.

Ray's buddies wound down their window and shouted at her to stop. When she didn't comply, they resorted to yelling obscenities and threats, joined by Ray. Peas in a pod. The scum of the earth. Undeterred, Dylan kept her gaze fixed ahead, though she covertly watched them from the corner of her eyes.

Anger washed across Ray's face, and he swerved toward her. Panic flared in Dylan's breast, and she jerked the wheel to the side. The tires squealed as she fought for control, the truck looming large beside her. Despite her best efforts to be brave, she was deathly afraid.

Ray pulled back just before he hit her vehicle, a smirk adorning his face. "Pull over. It's your only chance!"

Dylan squeezed her eyes shut, her knuckles turning white on the wheel. "Please, God. Don't let them get me."

"Come on now. Don't be like that. All we want is a little bit of fun."

Bile stung the back of Dylan's throat. She hated feeling helpless. It reminded her of the system, of everyone who'd wielded the power of life and death over her, and the foster dad who thought he could take what he wanted when he wanted. "Not again. Never again."

Anger flared in her gut, washing away the fear she felt. A sense of recklessness overtook her. She'd be damned if she gave in to these assholes. She'd never let them have the pleasure of taking her alive. She'd rather die. *What have I got to lose anyway? I'm dead already — a zombie.*

"Pull over, bitch," Ray yelled, growing impatient.

"Fuck off," she yelled back, giving him the middle finger.

"You'll pay for that," Ray screamed, his face turning purple with rage.

He swerved at her again, cutting it much closer this time.

Dylan jerked the wheel to the side. Her front tire hit a patch of gravel and skidded off the road. The car zigzagged wildly, bouncing over tussocks of grass and stones the size of her fists. A cloud of dust enveloped her and Ray's truck, obscuring the way ahead.

Dylan fought with the wheel, trying to get back onto the road. She narrowly missed hitting a tree, skidding sideways on the loose sand. She managed to regain control and jammed her foot onto the accelerator. The engine whined as she shot ahead of Ray and back onto the tar.

He followed, filling her rear window with the hulking silhouette of his truck. Dylan cried out when he nudged her with his bumper. The car jolted forward and almost careened into a deep ditch formed by run-off from the rains.

He came at her again, intent on ramming her. She swung to the opposite side of the road, narrowly escaping getting clipped. Ray increased his speed, once more drawing level with her. His friends hooted at her through their open window, and one let off a wild shot that narrowly missed.

Dylan was fast running out of options when she spotted a bend in the road ahead. A plan formed in her mind, and she prayed it would work. If it didn't, she was doomed. Honking the horn, she sought to grab the attention of all three her attackers.

Their heads turned toward her as one, eyebrows raised, and she yelled as loudly as she could. "Come and get me, you pieces of shit. I dare you!"

Ray's eyes narrowed to slits. "If you say so, bitch!"

For the third time, he came at her, yanking the wheel to the side. At the same time, Dylan slammed her foot on the brakes as hard as she could. The tires screamed, and the smell of burning rubber filled the air as the car squealed to a stop. Her body flew forward with the momentum, and her forehead connected with the steering wheel. Stars filled her eyes, and she blinked furiously to clear her vision.

Ray's truck shot past her and swung into the space where

she used to be. Taken by surprise, he lost control, weaving drunkenly from side to side. Within seconds, they'd reached the bend. Unable to turn in time, Ray's truck shot straight across and into a clump of thick vegetation on the other side.

With a loud crash, the truck's nose hit a tree dead-on. The screech of twisting metal and shattering glass filled the air as the engine and radiator imploded. A cloud of dust enveloped the scene, and steam rose from the hood, curling upwards in lazy swirls.

Dylan stared at the scene. One hand felt for the gun on the seat next to her. It was gone. It shot forward when she slammed on the brakes. She searched for it with frantic haste. She doubted the accident had taken care of Ray and his buddies for good. That lucky she hadn't been in a long time.

She spotted the weapon in the footwell and scooped it up before jumping out of the car. Her head swam, and her ears buzzed, but she forced herself to walk toward Ray's truck. With the gun at her side, and one hand pressed to her throbbing forehead, she stumbled forward. As she drew closer, the passenger side door opened, and one of Ray's friends fell out of the cab. He landed with a grunt, clearly disorientated.

Dylan squared her feet and raised the gun. This was her chance to even the odds. She squeezed off two shots but missed. "Damn it!"

She tried and missed again, her vision wavering. A sob escaped her lips, but she refused to give up. One more bullet. That was all she had left. *Better make it count, Dylan.*

She focused on her target and gripped the gun with both hands to steady her aim. Blowing out a slow breath, she pulled the trigger. This time, she didn't miss. Ray's friend, whoever he was, slumped to the ground with only half a skull. "Yes!"

Dylan bared her teeth in a grin of triumph. Her blood was up, and rage flowed through her veins igniting every cell in her body. Feverish heat flushed her cheeks, and she strode forward with renewed strength. It didn't matter that she was out of bullets. She didn't care. All she cared about was killing.

She reached the truck and stared at the body on the ground without remorse. "You got what you deserved, asshole."

Dylan stepped over the corpse and peered inside the cab still holding the Glock in her right hand. Ray was unconscious and lay slumped over the wheel, his limbs slack. It looked like he was pinned in place by crumpled metal, his legs broken and bleeding. Discounting him for the moment, she turned her attention to his buddy.

Ray's friend was groaning with both hands pressed to a gash on his scalp. It bled profusely like head wounds tended to do, and the metallic taste of blood coated the inside of her mouth. Her nostrils flared as she relished the aroma, and her stomach clenched with sudden hunger.

Her vision darkened around the edges, and the world appeared washed in crimson. Before she could stop to think, Dylan dropped her gun and grabbed him with both hands. "Not so cocky now, are we?"

"Let go, you crazy bitch," he mumbled, swatting at her with his fists

She didn't feel a thing, his blows no more than the buzzing of insects. Her focus narrowed onto his face, and she sneered. "I thought you wanted to have a little bit of fun. Aren't we having fun yet?"

He shook his head, eyes wide with fear when he looked into her eyes. Eyes that spelled out his death. "Lemme go, lemme go. Please!"

Dylan laughed, her gaze flickering to his throat. It looked soft and inviting. Vulnerable. With a growl, she lunged forward and sank her teeth deep into his jugular. Blood spurted into her mouth and washed across her tongue. Hot, fresh, and oh so delicious.

Her eyes drifted shut as ecstasy overcame her, and she sucked down deep mouthfuls of the warm fluid. Her victim thrashed beneath her, his horrified screams turning into gurgles as his life left him in a crimson stream.

Dylan's eyes snapped open when he stilled, and his struggles grew weaker and weaker. She tossed him aside like a rag doll, one hand wiping away the blood that ran down her chin. It covered the front of her jersey in a red waterfall, and she sniffed at it with disgust. "Ugh. So messy." She sighed. "And I just had a shower."

A frightened voice drew her attention, and her gaze traveled to Ray. He stared at her with wide eyes, and his voice shook when he asked, "What the hell are you?"

"What am I?" Dylan asked. "I'm your worst nightmare."

He attempted to pull his gun from its holster, but Dylan reacted in a flash. She leaned over and snatched it away.

Ray shook his head and pushed open his door. "You're a monster."

He struggled in his seat, attempting to climb out, but it was futile. He was pinned in place by the engine block.

"Oh, dear. It seems like you're stuck," Dylan said. "I'd help, but you know, I'm just a monster. Besides, I don't think there's much anybody could do for you now."

Ray gaped down at his broken legs, aware of his awful injuries for the first time. "Oh, God. Help me, please. I don't want to die."

"You should've thought of that before," Dylan said as she searched the cab for more weapons. Both his friends had been armed with handguns plus they'd brought along a rifle. "Nice stash. Thanks."

Afterward, she fished inside her pockets for her cigarettes and lighter. She hadn't had one in a long time.

Dylan lit one with relish and inhaled the acrid smoke deep into her lungs. Ray kept begging for help, but she ignored him as she searched the back of the truck until she found what she was looking for. A jerry can.

Opening the nozzle, she poured gas over the truck with methodical care. Ray watched with growing fear and realization. "No! No, please."

"Oh, yes."

"You can't do that. Please! I'll do anything, I swear it," he screamed. "Just name it, and I'll do it."

"The only thing I want from you is to die," was her cold reply.

Dylan stepped back and flicked the remains of her cigarette onto the ground next to a puddle of gas. With a swoosh, the fumes caught alight, and flames raced along the path she'd laid.

Ray continued pleading, but his blubbering cries soon turned into agonized screams when the fire enveloped the cab. He twisted and turned as his flesh blackened in the searing heat, his clothes, and hair a blazing inferno.

Dylan watched for a couple of seconds before turning away. The fire was as hot on the outside as she felt on the inside. A boiling pit of lava sat inside her stomach, ready to erupt at any moment. It made her feel strong, invincible, and she liked it.

With determined strides, she walked back to her car, taking her new weapons with her. She tucked Ray's fully loaded Beretta into her holster and stored the rest of the handguns in the glove compartment. The rifle she placed on the backseat. Then it was time to go.

As Dylan moved to start the engine, she caught sight of her reflection in the rearview mirror and froze. Her face was covered with drying blood, her teeth stained red, and her clothes soaked. The eyes of a stranger stared back at her, cold and callous.

In an instant, Dylan's mind cleared, and the haze of blazing fury that had fueled her so far faded away. She pressed one hand against her lips and choked back a horrified sob. "Oh, my God. What have I done?"

The sensation of blood flowing down her throat returned with awful clarity, and her stomach rebelled. She pushed the car door open and fell onto her hands and knees, not caring when sharp stones cut into her palms. Her body heaved, and copious amounts of blood splashed onto the road, the congealing fluid as black as tar.

With a cry, Dylan got to her feet and ran to the trunk. Along the way, she ripped off her soaked jersey and tossed it aside. Grabbing a bottle of water from her precious supplies, she washed the blood from her hands and face. Every time she caught sight of Ray's truck blazing in the distance, she retched. That carried on until she had nothing left in her stomach but bile and acid. Even then, the echo of his screams rang in her ears, over and over until she thought she'd go crazy.

Finally, she collapsed into a little ball. "I can't believe I did that. How could I do that? I'm a monster. A cannibal."

She stared at her hands, turning them this way and that. Her gaze traveled to the bandaged bite wound on her arm, and she traced the black veins to her chest. Realization dawned. "It's the infection. It's making me act all crazy. That's what it is."

136

Dylan checked the watch on her wrist. Forty-two hours remained. "I'm on the second day. From here on, it'll just get worse and worse. The fever, the veins, the psychotic episodes. If I want the cure, I'd better get moving. I have to get there before I'm too far gone to act human anymore."

She got to her feet, feeling weak and shaky. Her forehead burned, and her cheeks were flushed. The virus was progressing, working its way through her insides as her body attempted to fight it off.

From here, it was a straight shot to Louisville and then Fort Knox. She had a full tank, some supplies, and no one on her trail to stop. "I can do this. I have to. Louisville, here I come."

Chapter 21 - Amy

Amy shifted in her seat as they got closer to the Robinson farm, impatient to get there. The longer it took, the more worried she grew about Alex. He hadn't complained once, but she could see what the effort of driving cost him. It was evident in the stark lines around his mouth and the pallor of his cheeks. *If only he weren't so stubborn. I can drive. Not very well, but well enough to get us there.*

It was cold so early in the morning, and overcast. It would probably rain later on. She wondered how long they had left before winter hit them with its full force. Usually, the worst weather lasted from December to February, but this season promised to come early, and it was the beginning of November already.

Ordinarily, Amy loved winter, and some of her favorite memories stemmed from the season. In the evenings, they'd get together in the living room, each snuggled up underneath a fluffy blanket with a cup of steaming hot cocoa. Her father would read his latest book while she and her mom watched their favorite shows on television. All while a pot of soup bubbled on the stove, ready to be eaten with homemade crusty bread and real butter. A real treat.

Now, Amy wasn't so sure. Surviving during the warm

months would be difficult enough, but winter could be a killer. She sighed. That didn't matter now. They'd figure all of that out later. All that mattered now was getting Alex well again. *I hope Mr. and Mrs. Robinson can help him. I really do.*

"The turn-off is right ahead," Alex said, drawing Amy away from her morbid thoughts.

She craned her head and spotted the sign Alex referred to. It showed the way to the Robinson farm, a two-mile-long dirt road to the gates of their property.

On either side of the track, rows of tall trees loomed large above them. To Amy, they looked stark and foreboding, their naked branches twisting up to the gray clouds that covered the sky. A shiver worked down her spine despite the warm jacket she wore, and she wished the journey was over already. Something was bothering her, but she couldn't put her finger on it. *Nerves. It must be nerves.*

The dirt road wound through the woods for another mile before they reached the gates leading to the Robinson's property. Amy frowned, and Alex came to an abrupt halt as they surveyed the wreckage of the once elegant, wrought-iron gates that swung inward at the push of a button. They'd been forced open, and the metal was bent and warped on the inner seam where the two gates met.

"This can't be good," Amy said, clutching her shotgun to her chest.

"No, it can't," Alex agreed.

"Look at that," Amy said, pointing at the ground in front of them. The soil was churned up as if a hundred of pairs of feet had marched through it minutes before. "Those are prints. Footprints. And they're fresh."

"You're right," Alex said. "A whole lot of people came through here not long ago, and they must've forced open the gate."

"People? Or zombies?" Amy asked.

Suddenly, she realized what had been bothering her all along. A nature lover, she was used to tracking animals in the wild, and her subconscious mind had spotted these prints from the moment they turned onto the track.

"It could be either. The Robinson's are well off, and there are plenty of people who want what they have, but this…this was zombies. I'm sure of it," Alex replied.

"How come?"

"Because they forced open the gates. Thieves would have climbed over."

"So, what now?" Amy asked. "We can't go back home. We need medicine for you."

"It's too risky. Ten to one, the zombies are still here, unless the Robinson's managed to fight them off. But if that's the case, why is the property still open and exposed?"

"Maybe they're trapped and need our help," Amy said.

"What can we do against a horde of the undead, Amy?" Alex asked.

"We can at least look," Amy protested. "I mean, we're safe inside the car."

Alex stared ahead for a moment before nodding. "Fine. We can look, but at the first sign of trouble I'm getting us the hell out of here."

"Deal," Amy said.

Alex drove through the gates at a snail's pace, the tires crunching on the gravel driveway that led to the house. Within seconds, it came into view — a grand, two-story mansion set on a vast swath of green lawn. The wrap-around porch commanded a panoramic view of the countryside around it, and Amy leaned forward in her seat with anticipation.

Within moments, her hopes of finding the Robinson's alive and well were dashed. Mrs. Robinson's award-winning rose bushes had been trampled to dust, the regal plants crushed into the earth beneath countless feet. The grounds were littered with corpses, and the front door hung loose on broken hinges. The lower level windows were all smashed, and blood stained the once pristine white walls. It was like something out of her worst nightmares.

Amy's mouth dried up, and her heart was heavy in her chest. Tears pricked at her eyelids, but she dashed them away before Alex could see. She didn't want him to think her weak. "It was zombies."

Alex nodded, his face drawn. "They put up one helluva fight."

Amy had nothing to say to that. What did it matter when they were all dead?

"We'd better go. There's nothing here for us but death. Who knows where the rest of the horde is," Alex said.

Amy swallowed hard on the bile that rose in her throat. She could guess where the infected were. They'd be after food. Fresh meat. "The stables."

Alex glanced at her with a quizzical frown. "Stables?"

"At the back of the house, there's a row of stables for the racehorses. Mr. Robinson breeds them for the Kentucky Derby. There's a duck pond too. It used to be very pretty."

"Oh, God. Those poor animals."

Amy nodded, and her voice was faint when she spoke. "Let's go."

Alex reached over to squeeze her hand. "I'm sorry, Amy. I really am."

"I know."

As Alex prepared to make a U-turn, Amy stared at the house, grief for the Robinson family weighing heavily on her heart. Suddenly, she spotted something in one of the upper-story windows, and cried, "Wait, I saw something!"

"What?" Alex slammed on the brakes.

"Up there, in the window," Amy said, narrowing her eyes for a better look.

As she watched, the curtain twitched before it was swept aside to reveal a frightened face. It was a little girl, waving frantically at Amy and Alex.

Amy gasped. "It's Laura."

"Laura?" Alex asked.

"The Robinson's granddaughter," Amy cried out. "We have to rescue her!"

Before she could stop to think, Amy was out of the car and running toward the house. The only thought in her mind was to save that poor little girl before she could get eaten.

"Amy, no!" Alex shouted behind her, but she barely heard him. Instead, she dodged the bodies that littered the lawn and dashed into the house. Inside, it was chaos. Broken glass, furniture, and more bodies lay strewn about. Bullet holes graffitied the walls, and blood soaked the carpets.

Amy clapped one horrified hand to her mouth, but she didn't stop. She'd only been inside the house once, but she still remembered where the stairs were. She crossed the foyer and living room in a mad dash to the steps, taking them two at a time.

On the second floor, she paused, heaving for breath. On either side stretched a long hallway filled with doors. Taking a chance, she shouted, "Laura?"

One of the doors cracked open, and a pair of frightened blue

142

eyes stared at her. Amy almost fainted with relief. "Laura, it's me, Amy. You don't know me very well, but I'm here to help you."

Laura stared at her for a second before nodding. "Okay."

Amy reached out one trembling hand. "Come with me, sweetie. We have to leave before more zombies come."

Behind her sounded Alex's heavy tread on the stairs, his angry grunts harsh to her ears. She shot him a glance and pressed one finger to her lips. "Shh, you'll scare her."

He shot her a murderous look. "When we get out of here…"

"Yeah, yeah. You can do whatever you want then," Amy said, turning back to Laura, who'd inched her way outside the room she'd been hiding in. "Come on, sweetie. Time to go."

"What about Momma? And everyone else?" Laura asked.

"We'll look for them later, okay? But right now, we need to get out of here," Amy said.

"Alright." Laura ran to Amy and slipped her tiny hand into hers. "I'm ready."

"Thank God," Alex exclaimed with one last hard look at Amy. "I hope she's got better sense than you do."

"She's made it this far," Amy said, flashing him a cheeky grin. "Lead the way, big brother."

***

At the back of the house, an infected woman raised her head from the delicious feast before her. Blood dripped down her chin, rich and vital. Horse blood. It smeared across the name tag still affixed to her shirt, obliterating her name.

Anne.

That was who she used to be, back in the day when she still wore court shoes, painted her nails, and curled her hair. Back when she hated her job in telesales, counting the days until she could resign and marry a wealthy landowner. She'd even picked out her dream wedding dress already. The venue too. Everything was ready. She just had to meet her future husband-to-be and reel him in.

But now, Anne no longer cared about weddings or riches. Nor did she wear shoes anymore. They'd fallen along the wayside. A nuisance that slowed her down. Her hair hung lank and stringy against her decaying scalp, and her nails were broken to the quick.

Her head twitched as she listened for a repeat of the sound she'd just heard. Nothing. All she heard was her fellow zombies crunching on animal carcasses. Just when she was about to take another bite of horse entrails, she heard it again. "Amy, wait!"

Growling in anticipation, she pushed away from the already cooling flesh of the horse beneath her. Sound meant life, and life meant food. It was what she lived. Craved for. Died for.

Chapter 22 - Alex

Alex walked down the stairs in a hot temper. He was so angry at his sister that he almost missed the sound of bare feet slapping on tiled floors. He froze mid-step and raised one hand to Amy and Laura, who thankfully remained dead quiet.

A cacophony of growls broke the silence, and the tramping of a couple of feet became the march of many. His eyes widened when he realized what was coming their way, and he knew they'd never make it to the car. "Back, go back!"

Alex turned around and hustled the girls up the stairs, praying there was a way out for them. Or at least, a safe place they could hide.

Laura didn't dawdle, rushing back to her previous hiding spot with a shrill scream of terror. Amy followed, with Alex taking up the rear, his wound forgotten for the moment.

They climbed the last of the steps just as the horde reached the bottom, their hungry cries spurring them on. Together, they slipped inside Laura's bedroom and slammed the door shut.

Seconds later, many fists banged on the door until it sounded like a beating drum. The wood splintered around the lock and hinges. It wouldn't last very long. Alex cast around for an answer and spotted a massive chest of drawers. "Help me!"

He pushed the object toward the entrance, joined by Amy. They slid it in front of the bulging door, then added everything and anything they could lay their hands on: a toy box, chair, mirror, the lot.

Heaving for breath, Alex stood back to examine their handiwork. It wasn't enough, but it would buy them time. Time to figure out how to escape.

He rushed toward the window and looked out onto the front lawn. There stood their car. So close, yet impossibly far. The ground beckoned below, but jumping would yield them nothing but broken bones.

Unlatching the window, he pushed it wide open and leaned out. Beneath the sill was a wooden flower box filled with tiny white blooms. To the left, a gutter ran down from the roof to the bottom. It was just out of reach, but if they used the flower box as a step, they might make it.

He pressed on the box, checking how securely it was bolted to the wall. It seemed like it could hold, but they were taking a massive risk, especially with Laura. *I'll have to piggyback her. She'll never be able to do the climb on her own.*

He eyed Amy's slender form and wondered if she'd make it. She was strong and used to climb like a monkey when she was younger, but that was years ago. Still, they had no choice. If they stayed, they died.

Alex reached a hand toward Amy. "Come on. You first."

"What?"

"You heard me. We're getting out of here before those zombies bust down that door."

She leaned over the windowsill, and her face turned ashen. "That's suicide. There's nowhere to go."

"Yes, there is," Alex replied, acutely aware of the banging

behind them. It was growing louder by the second."Onto the flower box, then down the gutter. Go."

Amy shook her head. "I can't. I'm afraid of heights."

Alex ground his teeth in frustration and gripped her elbow. "Do you hear that sound? It's the sound of a horde of zombies waiting to strip the flesh from our bones."

Amy's eyes grew wild. "I…I know that."

"Do you? Because if you'd stopped to think for even one second, we wouldn't be in this mess in the first place." Alex's anger at his sister burst free, and he allowed it full reign.

"That's not fair. I had to save Laura," Amy protested.

"We could've come up with a plan, Amy. Not a wild dash to our certain deaths. This isn't a movie, and you're not some brave heroine out to save the day. This is real life."

"I…I'm sorry," Amy whispered as tears began to run down her cheeks.

Alex sighed, his anger leaving him in a rush. "I'm sorry. I didn't mean it like that, but if you don't go, we'll all die. I could never leave you."

Amy stared at him for a breathless moment. "Alright. This is my mess, and I have to fix it."

She climbed onto the windowsill, and gingerly stepped onto the flower box. It groaned but held beneath her weight. "What about my gun?" she asked, indicating the shotgun.

"Drop it."

She obeyed, and it clattered to the ground below. She leaned over and gripped the gutter with both hands before swinging her legs over. For a single terrifying moment, she hung suspended in the air, her feet scrabbling for purchase. Alex held his breath, afraid she'd fall. But she found a foothold and began the slow climb down to the bottom.

Behind Alex, the door was giving way, the furniture shifting beneath the combined weight of so many bodies pressing against it. He turned to Laura. "Climb onto my back."

She didn't hesitate, clambering onto him like a squirrel. He climbed through the window and onto the box. It shifted, and he froze. "Please don't break. Please."

It held, and he reached for the gutter. It was smooth, hard to hold onto, but there were seams between the different sections. He clung to these with his fingertips and toes, lowering himself to the ground.

Laura held on, not making a sound, and he began to hope. That hope was shattered when the door inside the bedroom gave way to the infected. In an instant, the room was flooded with zombies. They oozed out of the window, reaching for them with hungry fingers.

Alex panicked. "Amy, are you down yet?"

"I am. You can come," she shouted back.

He closed his eyes and loosened his grip, sliding the rest of the way down. The ground came up too fast, and he landed hard. His right ankle twisted, and burning pain shot up his leg. "Fuck!"

A body tumbled past him, landing on the ground with a loud crunch of bone and cartilage. The infected were throwing themselves out the window. A blast nearly deafened him. It was Amy, wielding her shotgun. "Alex, run!"

He pushed himself up from the ground and grabbed Laura's hand. "Come on."

Together, they ran across the lawn, heading for the car. Amy danced ahead of them, firing off her last two shots. She pulled out her pistol next, the shots going wild.

Alex ran as fast as he could with his gimpy leg, dragging

Laura by the hand. He dared to look over his shoulder and instantly regretted it. Zombies were falling from the window like rain from the sky. Some fell on their heads, cracking open their skulls. Others broke their necks, becoming paralyzed. But they only provided a comfortable cushion to the rest that followed. They got up fast and sprinted after their chosen prey, running much more quickly than either Alex or Laura could.

They weren't going to make it, Alex realized in an instant, and his thoughts shot to Amy. She had to live. No matter what. "Amy, start the car!"

She shot him a wild look but obeyed, jumping behind the wheel and starting the engine. Alex sped up, forcing his broken body to move faster than was humanly possible. The distance between him and the car narrowed, and Amy leaned over to open the passenger side door.

Hope rose in his chest. Maybe they could make it after all. It was only a few more yards to safety. Laura's hand was sweaty, slipping against his palm, but he didn't let go. She had to keep pace. She had to. They were almost there. His gaze met Amy's, and she shouted something at him, but he couldn't hear the words.

Suddenly, Laura was yanked from his grip, and Alex stumbled to a halt. He looked back and screamed. An infected had hold of Laura, her tiny form hugged to his chest as if to comfort her. But comfort was the last thing on the zombie's mind. His teeth dug into her neck, right where the shoulder connected.

"No!" Alex cried, his insides liquefying at the terrible sight.

The zombie tore out a hunk of flesh, chewing with relish. Blood spurted from the wound, a red mist that covered them both in a spray of crimson fluid. Laura screamed, and it was a sound that Alex never forgot as long as he lived.

Other infected reached them and latched onto the little girl. They dug into her with their teeth and nails, tearing her limb from limb in a feeding frenzy.

Alex found himself frozen in the moment, unable to move. Then a hand tugged at his arm, and a shrill voice commanded him. "Alex, move! You have to move!"

His limbs moved on autopilot, and he stumbled to the waiting car. Amy ushered him inside and slammed the door shut. "Wait right there."

She dashed around the front and jumped in beside him. With a roar of the engine, she pulled away, leaving a cloud of dust in their wake.

Alex sat in his seat like a statue. He'd lost the little girl. She was just a child, and it was all his fault. In his mind's eye, he relived her death over and over again until it ran on a loop.

Amy shouted something at him, but he couldn't make out the words. Instead, a dark cloud descended over his eyes, and he leaned back in his seat without fighting it any longer. His body, weakened by infection and blood loss, gave up the struggle, and he sank into oblivion with a sigh of relief. Anything was better than hearing her screams.

Chapter 23 - Dylan

Dylan ducked her head as shots punched into her car. The windshield shattered, raining her with glass, and she swerved sideways to avoid the incoming hail of bullets. The front tire hit the pavement with terrific force and burst with a loud bang.

"Oh, crap, no!" Dylan shouted as she lost control and crashed into a fire hydrant. The nose of the car crumpled inward, and a jet of water shot into the air from the broken hydrant. The water poured back down onto the vehicle, drenching her within seconds, and obscuring her view.

Dylan twisted sideways and grabbed the duffel bag containing her food and water. She unzipped it with lightning speed and stuffed the rifle inside. Her empty Glock and one of the Beretta's she took from Ray, and his buddies followed. With the second pistol in her hand and Ray's gun in her holster, she jumped out of the car.

A bullet struck the tar next to her feet and ricocheted into the air with an ugly whine. Hunched low to the ground, Dylan ran toward the nearest shelter she could find. She wedged her body into a tiny gap between two recycling bins and took stock of the situation.

It was as bad as it could get.

Coming into Louisville had been a colossal mistake. She'd

have been better off sticking to the back roads and bypassing the city altogether. But she'd been in a rush. The clock was ticking, and even now, she only had around forty hours left to make it to Fort Knox. While it might sound like a lot, getting out of the city was proving impossible.

The city was a war zone. Posters stuck to every lamp post announced that an evacuation would take place that afternoon from the Churchill Downs racetrack located on Central Avenue. That meant every single able-bodied person in the city was fighting to get there, and most of them were armed and trigger-happy. Undead roamed the streets in packs, causing random shooting to break out. The streets ran red with the blood of both the infected and innocent civilians.

"I have to get out of here," Dylan muttered, searching for a means of escape. It seemed hopeless. Her car was totaled, and she'd never make it on foot.

A zombie spotted her and charged. Dylan raised her gun and fired three shots before scoring a head shot, and the thing collapsed mere feet away. A teen boy ran past with his skateboard tucked underneath one arm. He vaulted over the corpse without pause and continued down the street. A small family followed, the mother carrying her toddler on her hip with the father bringing up the rear.

Dylan jumped to her feet and entered the maelstrom, the duffel bag slung across her back. She couldn't afford to hide any longer. A truck swerved past her, so close its wake ruffled her clothes, and a rough elbow hit her in the ribs. She stumbled and fell to her knees, one hand bracing her fall. A boot stepped on her fingers, stomping the delicate digits into the ground.

Dylan hissed and yanked her hand away. Suckling on the injured area, she shoved her way through the desperate crowd.

Her ears rang from the noise, a hellish mixture of car horns, alarms, shouting, screaming, and crying. "Out of my way!"

From a side street, a group of infected attacked, and the people went wild, trampling each other in their haste to escape. Dylan fired at the zombies, missing as often as she scored. Within seconds, her gun was empty, and she shoved it into the top of her jeans with a curse. "Shit, I'm out!"

"Allow me," a man with a thick beard said as he let rip with an AK-47.

Several zombies went down, but he missed the undead woman that crept up behind him. She pounced onto his back and sunk her teeth into his neck. Blood spurted in a fountain of red, splashing onto Dylan's shirt. She aimed a quick shot at the zombified woman and hit her between the eyes. It was too late for the bearded man, however. He was a goner.

Dylan scooped up his AK-47, aimed it at the remaining undead, and pulled the trigger. A spray of bullets erupted from the weapon, cutting down the last of the infected. She was unprepared for the kick-back however and dropped the rifle with a cry as fiery pain shot through her injured fingers. "Ouch, that hurt, you m—"

She swallowed the rest of her sentence, aware that she was down to one gun unless she dipped into the duffel bag. Even then, she only had one more loaded handgun, and the rifle left. Besides, the rifle wouldn't be of much use in such close quarters.

Dylan pressed ahead, searching for a way out. There had to be something she could do, somewhere she could go. It didn't help that she was a stranger to the city, and none of the street names meant anything to her.

A pair of clawed hands latched onto her shoulders, and a

diseased face appeared in front of her, the mouth gaping. A rotten stench filled her nostrils, and Dylan fought to keep the snapping teeth out of her flesh.

A blade flashed through the air, narrowly missing Dylan and lodged in the infected's neck. Thick, black blood spurted from the wound caused by the machete, but the zombie barely paused. Instead, it lunged at its attacker, a well-meaning young man trying to save Dylan's life.

Having lost his weapon, the youngster became the victim as the infected latched onto his face. His gurgling screams were lost in the din, and Dylan had to fight to keep her spot in the surging crowd. She pulled her gun from its holster and shot the zombie in the head. One look at her rescuer showed her it was a lost cause, however. Blood bubbled up from a deep hole in his cheek, and more pumped from his neck. He'd be dead within seconds. Their eyes met, his wide and frantic, hers shocked and horrified.

"Kill me," he mumbled, bloody foam frothing on his lips. "I don't want to turn into one of them."

Dylan nodded. "I'm sorry."

She pulled the trigger one more time, ending his suffering. For a single moment, Dylan considered giving up. It'd be easy. All she had to do was turn the gun on herself, and it would all be over.

Gritting her teeth, she forced herself to carry on. She couldn't give up. Not now. Tucking the gun back into its holster, she grabbed the machete instead. She needed a hand weapon, and she had to save her ammunition.

Suddenly, a young teen girl appeared in front of Dylan, her blue eyes wild with terror. They fixed on Dylan's face, and she reached out a pleading hand. "Can you help me, please? It's my brother. He's hurt. I need to get him inside."

Dylan hesitated, then shook her head. "I'm sorry, but I need to get out of this city. I don't have time to waste."

She pushed past the girl who grabbed her hand and pleaded, "Please. I need you to help me carry him inside. He's in the car over there. It'll only take a moment."

Screams erupted behind them as another wave of the undead attacked the fleeing masses in the street, and Dylan pushed the girl into a dark alley. After checking that it was clear, she hunkered down behind a trash bin with the girl by her side.

"Car? You have a car?" Dylan asked, the wheels spinning in her head.

The girl stilled, and a calculating look entered her eyes. "You said you need to get out of the city, right?"

"That's right."

"Help me get my brother fixed up, and we'll take you wherever you need to go. He's a soldier, a fighter, and I can shoot too. Plus, he knows this city like the back of his hand. Together, we can make it."

"What's wrong with your brother?" Dylan asked.

"He was stabbed two days ago. We patched him up, but it's infected. He needs antibiotics," the girl replied.

"Where do we get that?" Dylan asked. "I haven't seen a pharmacy anywhere near here."

"There is a veterinary clinic three shops down," the girl replied, jerking her head back the way Dylan had come.

"A vet?" Dylan asked, amused. "I suppose it could work."

"It will work. I know what to look for. I spent last summer volunteering there, and I learned a couple of things."

"I see," Dylan said. "So, here's the deal. I'll help you get your brother safely into the clinic if you give me the keys to your car."

"No way," the girl replied. "You help me get him inside, fixed up again, and back to the car. Then I'll give you the keys, and we can all get out of here."

Dylan chewed on her bottom lip, thinking it over. It wasn't as if she had a lot of options open to her, and frankly, she needed the help. Finally, she nodded and stuck out her hand. "You drive a hard bargain, little girl, but it's a deal."

"I'm not a little girl. I'm sixteen, and my name is Amy."

"Alright, Amy. I'm Dylan. Nice to meet you. Now let's go save your brother."

They shook on it, and the bargain was struck.

Chapter 24 - Dylan

Dylan gripped the machete with both hands and peered out of the alley. The street had cleared somewhat as the people had run away with the latest horde of infected howling on their heels. She wasn't sure it was a blessing, though. The streets of Louisville were a horror, something from a different dimension, and the lack of crowds lay it bare for all to see.

Bodies lay sprawled out in the open, their eyes sightless and their faces frozen with terror. Blood congealed in puddles around them as the monstrosities that used to be human once fed on their flesh. Flies buzzed around these clusters of death in black clouds, drawn to the feast, and the scent of blood, offal, and decay was impossible to ignore.

Dylan swallowed hard to keep the contents of her stomach in place and turned to Amy. "Where's your car?"

Amy leaned out and pointed to a white sedan parked not far away. "It's that one. Alex is in the back seat."

"It's locked?"

"Of course. I'm not that stupid. What if someone tries to steal it while I'm gone?" Amy said.

"Do you have the keys?" Dylan asked.

Amy nodded. "I do."

"Give them to me. When we get there, you stand guard with

the shotgun while I open the car and haul your brother out."

Amy eyed her with cold blue eyes. "No offense, lady, but I don't know you. I'll unlock the door first, and then I'll stand guard while you get him out."

Dylan chuckled. "You're a smart one. I like that."

"What's the plan?" Amy asked.

"We run like hell and hope nothing without a pulse spots us," Dylan answered.

"That's not much of a plan," Amy said.

"Yeah, well. I'm not much of a planner. Let's go," Dylan said, dashing out of the alley.

She ran straight for the sedan, reaching it within seconds. She hunkered down next to it and was joined by Amy a moment later.

"Did any zombies spot us?" Amy asked, her head swiveling like an owl's.

Dylan took a careful look around. Cars pushed up the street, swerving around knots of feeding infected and crashed cars, while a steady trickle of people ran past them. These were mostly families or singles carrying their belongings, and she even spotted one lady with a parrot on her shoulder.

One heavily armed group jogged along the opposite pavement, heading to the evacuation zone. They were more organized than most with their senior members and children clustered in the center. They gunned down anything that looked like a threat, a bonus for Dylan. Most of the feeding infected had now focused their attention on this group, leaving Dylan and Amy in the clear. "Now's our chance."

Amy quickly unlocked the back door and opened it while Dylan peered inside. Sprawled on the seat lay a young man of solid build, and she wondered whether she'd be able to carry him by herself. "We'll just have to see, won't we?"

Dylan tucked her machete into her belt and leaned over to grab his shoulders. With Amy's help, she managed to lever him upright into a sitting position. Looping one arm around his back, she propped him onto her shoulder and heaved him upright.

By this point, Alex was semi-awake and doing his best to help with Amy's gentle prodding. "Come on, bro. You can do it. We can't carry you all by ourselves."

"I'm sorry," he mumbled, shuffling his feet forward in a semblance of a walk.

It was good enough for Dylan, who hustled him forward as fast as she could manage. She hated being out in the open and exposed like this. They reached the clinic doors, and Amy raised one hand to Dylan. "Wait here while I check inside."

Dylan glanced around, relieved to see they were in the clear for the moment. No one paid them much mind, and the infected had all fallen to the armed group's guns. "Okay, but hurry."

Amy shoved the doors open with one shoulder, her shotgun raised and ready for anything that might be inside. She disappeared for a few seconds, but to Dylan, it felt like forever. She glanced around nervously, shifting from one foot to the other.

Alex was growing heavier by the minute, his cooperation fading as he drifted in and out of consciousness. Even through his clothes, she could feel the fever blazing from his skin. His heat matched hers, and she became more aware of her own advancing infection. *He'd better be on his feet soon, or I'm taking those keys and leaving by myself.*

Amy returned at last and waved them inside. "It's clear."

Dylan rushed inside, never happier to hear the sound of doors being shut behind her. Amy dropped the blinds and pulled a heavy chair in front of the entrance, blocking it off. "That should hold us for a while."

"Alright. Where to now?" Dylan asked.

"Follow me," Amy said, leading the way to the waiting room where long leather couches lined the walls. "Put him on one of those."

Dylan shrugged Alex off with a sigh of relief, massaging her aching neck. "Man, he weighs a ton."

"I know. That's why I needed your help," Amy said, which Dylan could believe with the girl's petite build.

She eyed Alex's husky frame and dark hair, comparing it to the blonde, blue-eyed Amy. "You don't look like brother and sister."

"I take after my mom," Amy said. "Alex looks more like my dad."

"Where are they?" Dylan asked.

"Dead." The word came out flat, but the look of grief on the girl's face caused a pang of sympathy to rise in Dylan's heart. She regretted the question instantly. *I can't afford to feel sorry for them. Not if I might have to steal their car.*

"Where's the medicine?" she asked, changing the subject.

"I'll go get it. Just watch him, please. He's all I've got left," Amy replied before rushing off.

"Will do," Dylan said, squashing another jolt of regret for the girl. She liked Amy. The teen might be young and small of build, but she was tough, and no fool either. That was the problem. She couldn't afford to form attachments. Not with her injury.

After a couple of minutes, Amy showed up with an armful of

goods which she dumped onto an empty space on the couch. While she set to work sorting the stuff out, Dylan unslung her duffel bag and removed a bottle of water and a protein bar. She quickly ate the bar and downed the water with a handful of the pills Ethan had given her for the fever. It didn't feel like it was helping much, but at this stage, she figured anything was better than nothing.

She also checked the remaining bullets in her gun. The magazine was about half-full, and she still had one more loaded handgun and the rifle as a backup. The machete wasn't half-bad either. The blade was long and razor-sharp with a firm grip, but it was also coated in zombie blood.

"Ugh," she said with a shudder. "Is there a bathroom in here?"

Amy pointed at a door in the far corner. "Over there."

"Thanks. I'll be right back."

Dylan used the opportunity to empty her full bladder before cleaning the blade with soap and a towel. Afterward, she washed her face and hands too, feeling refreshed.

She returned to find Amy struggling to unwind Alex's bandages, and she stepped forward. "Here. Let me help."

With a pair of scissors, she cut through the cloth and propped him up so Amy could remove it. Together, they inspected the wound, and Dylan wrinkled her nose at the smell. "Ew. That's almost as bad as mine."

Amy threw her a questioning look. "Yours?"

Realizing she'd said too much, Dylan shrugged it off. "Uh, nothing. Don't worry about it. Let me clean up the cut while you ready the shot."

"Okay. I've got antibiotics and something for the pain and fever too. It's pretty strong, so he'll be out for a while."

"How long is a while?" Dylan asked. "I can't wait too long."

161

"A couple of hours, maybe. And don't think about ditching us, lady. Alex is your best shot at getting out of here. He knows this place better than most," Amy said.

Dylan groaned aloud. "Fine. Whatever. And the name's Dylan. Not lady."

"Whatever you say."

Dylan swallowed a sarcastic retort and turned her attention to Alex's injury. With clean gauze and antiseptic, she flushed out the wound and bandaged it. Afterward, she gave him the shot Amy handed her, relieved to find his veins were quite prominent. Once she was finished, she sat back on her heels. "I guess we can't do anything but wait, right?"

"Right," Amy said.

For the next three hours, Dylan paced up and down while Amy coddled her brother. She washed his brow with a wet cloth, fed him sips of water, and even found a fan in one of the offices to cool him down.

During a brief bathroom break, Dylan found herself eyeing Alex with a sour look. With every minute that passed, her impatience grew. She was down to roughly thirty-seven hours, and she wasn't feeling so hot herself. The only upside to the situation was the gradual emptying of the street outside. No doubt, people had reached the evacuation point with the sole exception of a few stragglers. Hopefully, they'd drawn most of the undead with them, leaving the way clear for Dylan and her group.

A frown formed between her brows. Since when were they part of her group? *It's too late. I've grown attached, damn it!*

"Maybe I should just smother you in your sleep," Dylan muttered to the sleeping Alex.

His eyebrows twitched, and a half-smile twisted his lips. "I heard that."

"You're awake?" She rushed to his side and pressed one hand to his forehead. "You're still hot, though. The fever hasn't fully broken."

"Maybe not, but I feel a lot better. It's not so painful anymore," he replied, pushing himself upright with a grunt.

"Here. Drink this," Dylan said, handing him a bottle of water.

"Thanks," Alex replied, chugging it all down in one big gulp. "Who are you?"

"The name's Dylan. I'm helping your sister out."

Amy returned from the bathroom and spotted him awake and lucid. She rushed over and hugged him tightly. "Alex! You're okay."

"Thanks to you and Dylan here," he replied.

"It's nothing. As long as you get me to Fort Knox within the next few hours, we're even," Dylan said.

"What's the rush?" Alex asked.

"That's for me to know," Dylan said, skirting the issue. After Maddie, she wasn't about to let people know she was infected again. Not unless she was sure she could trust them.

Amy shocked her with her next words, however. "You've been bitten, haven't you? You're infected."

"How did you know that?" Dylan asked, taking a defensive stand.

"I figured it out when you said his wound was almost as bad as yours. Besides, your veins are starting to show."

"Where?"

"In your neck."

Alex nodded. "I can see them too. How long have you got left?"

"A day and a half, roughly," Dylan answered. Now that the

cat was out of the bag, she might as well be honest with them. Besides, if they were going with her to Fort Knox, they'd better be aware of the risks.

"Are you having episodes yet?" Alex asked with a shrewd gaze.

"It's begun," Dylan admitted. "I'm dangerous."

"And you want us to take you to Fort Knox. Why there?" Alex asked.

"Because they've got a cure," Dylan said.

A shocked silence ensued.

"A cure? For real?" Alex asked.

"I can't believe it!" Amy said.

Dylan nodded. "It's not a joke. It's real, and I need to get it before it's too late."

"I see."

"Are you thinking of backing out?" Dylan asked.

"No. You helped us even though it could've cost you."

"It did cost me," Dylan pointed out. "Three hours and counting, to be precise."

Alex held up a placating hand. "Okay, okay. I get it. It cost you, and I owe you one for that."

"We keep our promises," Amy interjected.

"Great," Dylan said. "With that settled, can we go now?"

Alex peered at his watch. "I'm up for it on one condition."

"What's that?"

"I drive. With your infection, I can't trust you behind the wheel. What happens if you have an episode?"

"No problem. I'll ride shotgun," Dylan said, itching to go.

"You should eat something first, Alex," Amy protested. "You're still weak."

"I need to use the bathroom too," Alex said.

164

"And we should take some medicine with us," Amy said.

Dylan rolled her eyes and slumped down onto the nearest couch. "Fine. I'll wait, but hurry it up, damn it. I'm timing you."

Amy flashed her a dimpled smile. "You know. I think you're all bark and no bite."

"You do?" Dylan asked with raised eyebrows. "Then you're dumber than I thought."

"Or smarter," Amy replied, sticking out her tongue before flouncing off.

Dylan couldn't help but laugh a little. The girl had guts. Lots of it. Alex too. Injured as he was, he'd still committed to helping her — a man with integrity.

As she waited for her new posse to get ready, Dylan realized that she quite liked having company. She didn't have to cope on her own anymore, and that was a pretty awesome feeling.

Chapter 25 - Alex

Alex navigated the quieter streets of Louisville with old familiarity. His teen years were spent joy-riding with buddies after school and taking girlfriends to secret spots. During his adult years, the few times that he'd been granted a pass, he'd had more appreciation for the place of his birth. He'd explored its every nook and cranny, relishing in its combination of old-school charm, history, and progressive energy.

It wasn't like that now. The streets were deserted, empty. Those who could had made their way to the Churchill Downs racetrack for evacuation and the dead had followed the trail of fresh meat like the predators they'd become. Those who couldn't, or wouldn't leave the city, were holed up inside their barricaded homes.

Dusk had fallen, painting the buildings in hues of gray and charcoal. No longer would the skyline light up with bright lights, ready to welcome the young and energetic. All that was gone now. Light, sound, and smell was the enemy for it drew the dead like moths to a flame. It had been threatening to rain all day, and now the first fat drops hit the windshield.

Alex left his home behind with a glimmer of regret. He'd miss the place, but there was no use in looking back. As the rain drummed onto the roof of the car, wrapping them in a cocoon of rhythmic sound, he glanced at Amy in the backseat. "What happened, Amy? After the Robinson's?"

She glanced at him before looking down at her lap again. "I went to Louisville looking for medicine. I figured it was your only chance. Then I met Dylan, and you know the rest."

"That was brave of you. You saved my life."

She shook her head. "I'm not brave. I'm stupid. If it weren't for me, Laura would still be alive."

A pang of pain and regret shot through his heart at the mention of Laura, but there was no point in dwelling on it. If he did, it would drive him mad. "You can't think like that, Amy. You made a mistake. It happens. You can't win all the time. Learn from it."

"That poor little girl," Amy whispered. "I just wanted to help her. Instead, I killed her."

"It's not your fault, Sis. Believe me. I'm sorry you had to see that, but at least you kept your head on straight. If you hadn't dragged my ass out of there, I'd be dead too."

"I suppose," Amy said with a sniff.

"You're stronger than you know. You're a fighter, and you'll get over this in time. I promise," Alex said.

Dylan twisted around in her seat. "It's called ripping off the band-aid. Face what happened, admit your mistakes, try to learn from the experience, and honor Laura's memory by becoming a better person."

Amy stared at her. "I'll try."

"That's pretty deep," Alex said, eyeing his new traveling partner. To date, she remained a mystery, not revealing anything about herself.

Dylan snorted. "I'd better believe in my own advice, or I'd go nuts."

"How so?"

"I tore out a man's throat with my teeth this morning and drank his blood. After that, I set his friend on fire and watched him burn."

Alex blinked, taken aback by her brutal honesty. "Good God, I can see how that would haunt a person."

"Exactly."

She glanced at him with those enigmatic blue-green eyes. They were an unusual shade, complimented perfectly by her dark red hair. He wondered what lurked behind them. A monster? Or simply a woman on the brink of succumbing to a viral infection. That remained to be seen.

He patted his pocket. At least, he had brought insurance with him in case she had another episode. Amy had spotted them. Horse tranquilizers. Those in the process of turning often displayed incredible strength and aggression, plus they still had their intelligence. That made them doubly dangerous, and he couldn't take any chances with Amy in the car.

"Why don't you two try and get some sleep? We'll be there before you know it. About an hour," Alex suggested. Ordinarily, he could make the drive in half the time, but it was raining, and he couldn't see very far ahead in the murky darkness.

Dylan and Amy agreed, and within a few minutes, both were fast asleep. A peaceful silence descended on the vehicle, and Alex was able to relax at last. He glanced at the map on his lap and hoped Dylan was right about the cure. It would suck getting there, only to find out it was nothing more than a mirage.

***

They were about halfway to their destination when Dylan came awake with a start. She looked around her with a confused expression. "Who am I? Where am I?"

Alex stared at her for a second. "You don't remember?"

She shook her head. "No."

In the backseat, Amy woke up as well. "What's going on?"

"I'm not sure," Alex admitted.

"I'm hungry," Dylan said. "In fact, I'm starving."

"Will a protein bar do the trick?" Amy asked, rummaging in Dylan's duffel bag.

"Sure."

Amy handed her the bar, and Alex watched with fascination as she ripped into it like it was a hunk of meat. Within seconds it was gone. "More. I'm still hungry."

Amy gave her another bar and a packet of potato chips which she promptly tore into.

"Man, you are hungry, huh?" Alex said.

Dylan didn't even acknowledge him, and a frisson of fear worked its way down his spine. Something wasn't right about her. Was she having an episode again? He remembered what she'd told them about her last one, and he decided he didn't want to risk it. "Why don't we stop and stretch our legs. I could use a quick break."

"But, it's raining," Amy protested.

"It stopped awhile ago, Sis. Besides, I really think we should stop," he said, throwing meaningful looks at the still eating Dylan.

Amy's eyes widened as she caught his drift. "Okay, sure."

He pulled over, and after a careful look around, he got out. Dylan stayed in her seat, occupied with her chips. Amy sidled up next to him and whispered, "It's an episode, isn't it?"

"I think so. We'd better put her under." Alex pulled out a vial of the tranquilizers. With Amy's help, he drew up a syringe.

Just enough to knock out a grown man, not enough to kill her. She'd be stronger than most humans and resistant to the drug because of the virus. He's learned that much from the army.

He was about to get back into the car and stick it in her arm when a low growl sounded behind him. The hair on the back of his neck rose. "Amy. Get in the car."

"But—"

"Now," he commanded.

She slipped away, and he waited for Dylan to make her move. A crunch of gravel was the only warning he got before she tackled him from behind. She hit him like a ton of bricks, and they both went down hard. His teeth slammed shut, and blood filled his mouth as he bit his tongue. *Bitch.*

Crazed or not, she was going down. He'd managed to keep hold of the syringe, but the real problem was keeping her teeth out of his flesh. She snapped at his neck, getting a mouthful of leather jacket each time. Working one hand underneath him, he bucked his hips violently and tossed her into the air.

Dylan was thrown to the side where she landed with a yelp of surprise. He launched himself across her body, pinning her to the ground. She wriggled like a worm on a hook, growling the entire time.

Alex searched for a patch of open skin to stick the needle in, but she didn't give him a chance. Her one hand shot free, and she raked at his scalp with her fingernails, drawing blood. Alex yelled in pain, unable to get up for fear she'd get a bite in.

Suddenly, Amy was there. She grabbed Dylan's free hand and yanked up her sleeve. "There! Do it now!"

Alex jabbed the needle into Dylan's exposed forearm and injected the tranquilizer. She snarled, her struggles growing worse for a brief moment, and he hoped the medicine was strong enough. "Please work. Please work."

It did.

Bit by bit, she quieted. The growls ceased, replaced by soft mewls. Her muscles slackened until she lay like a rag doll, and her eyes drifted shut. Within seconds, she was fast asleep, her breath whistling in and out of her lungs at a rhythmic pace.

Alex slumped with relief. "Thank God."

He eased himself off her, wincing at the fresh pain in his side. The struggle had torn open the wound, and it was bleeding all over again. "Ah, crap. Look at that."

"It's okay," Amy said. "I'll patch you up quickly, but we'd better get to the Fort. You both need proper attention."

"Agreed," Alex said, heaving the limp form of Dylan into the backseat. "The sooner we get there, the better."

After Amy performed her magic, Alex hit the road again, propped up by another shot of painkillers. These weren't strong enough to knock him out, just dulling the worst, so he was able to function.

They'd gone past Radcliff, and he took the road leading to the Fort. He was wondering what he'd find there when he spied a barricade across the way. Not just any roadblock. An army blockade complete with tactical vehicles including a light tank and a small building to the side. A high, chain-link fence stretched into the distance on either side, and gate blocked the way through. Floodlights brightly lit the entire area, and armed guards patrolled the area.

Alex slowed, approaching the waiting soldiers with caution. They watched him come closer, their rifles held across their bodies in a position of readiness but not an outward threat.

One approached his window and asked in polite tones. "Can we help you, Sir? This is a private military institution."

"I...um...I thought this was a safe zone? For civilians?" Alex asked.

"Are you seeking entry?" the soldier asked, staring into the car at Amy who watched with wide-eyed wonder.

"Yes, we are," Alex answered.

"Who are you?"

"My name is Alex Donahue, nobody special, Sir. This is my sister Amy," Alex said.

"And that?" The soldier pointed at the snoring Dylan, his mouth quirking at the corners. "She's real tired, isn't she?"

"Actually, we found her in Louisville, where she helped us out. Her name is Dylan. Not sure of the last name."

"Are any of you injured? Infected with the Vita virus?" the soldier asked.

Alex hesitated. Now that they were here, he wasn't so sure of their reception. "I've been stabbed, Sir."

"Stabbed?"

"Yeah, a couple of guys tried to rob me."

"I see. Anything else? And you might as well be honest. Lying won't get you anywhere," the soldier said.

"It's the girl, Dylan. She's infected, but we have her tranquilized as a precaution," Alex said, hoping he hadn't doomed her. "We heard you have a cure here. Is that true?"

"Where was she bitten, and how long ago?" the soldier asked, ignoring Alex's question.

"On the arm, and it was about a day and a half ago," Alex said. "Thirty-five hours, or so."

"You're sure about that?"

"Yes, Sir. She told us all about it," Amy interrupted.

The soldier smiled. "Well, she's in luck. If she'd gone over forty-eight hours, it'd have been too late."

The soldier pointed at the massive steel gate. "Go on through, but be warned. Once you're inside, you'll have to give up all your guns and supplies. No hoarding. We share everything here. Got that?"

"Yes, Sir. I understand." While Alex didn't relish giving up his weapons, Dylan needed that cure. If that was the price they'd have to pay, so be it.

The soldier tipped his head and stepped aside. "Welcome to Fort Knox."

Epilogue

"Aren't we having fun yet?"

"Lemme go, lemme go. Please!"

Dylan laughed, her gaze flickering to her victim's throat. It looked soft and inviting. Vulnerable. With a growl, she lunged forward and sank her teeth deep into his jugular. Blood squirted into her mouth and washed across her tongue. Hot, fresh, and oh so delicious.

Her eyes drifted shut as ecstasy overcame her, and she sucked down deep mouthfuls of the warm fluid. Her victim thrashed beneath her, his horrified screams turning into gurgles as his life left him in a crimson stream.

Dylan's eyes snapped open when he stilled, and his struggles grew weaker and weaker. She tossed him aside like a rag doll, one hand wiping away the blood that ran down her chin.

She turned in a slow circle, surveying the field she stood in. Corpses lay strewn around her feet. More than she could count. Their empty eyes stared sightlessly into the distance. The grass swayed in the breeze, tipped with red.

A field of blood.

A field of death.

Movement caught her gaze, and she whirled to find Ethan standing a few feet away. He pointed an accusing finger at her. "You did this."

"No." Dylan shook her head in a futile denial.
"You're a monster."
"No!"
"A cannibal."
"I'm sorry, I didn't mean to."
"A zombie!"
***

"Wake up, Dylan. You're dreaming. Wake up!"

An insistent hand shook her shoulder, and she shot upright with a gasp. Sweat poured from her brow, and her shirt clung to her damp skin. Shirt? No. It wasn't a shirt. It looked more like a hospital gown.

She twisted from side to side, taking in her strange surroundings. She was lying in a bed tucked into a small, curtained cubicle. It smelled of antiseptic, and everything came in shades of white.

White curtains, white tiled floors, white linen, and a white doctor's lab coat. The doctor in question stepped closer, holding a clipboard. "Calm down, Dylan. It was just a nightmare. You're safe now. I promise."

Dylan blinked. "Safe?"

"Yes. I'm Dr. Tara Lee, and you're in the infirmary at Fort Knox. You came here seeking the cure."

"The cure?" The fog cleared from Dylan's head, and she nodded. "Yes, the cure."

"How did you hear about it, if I may ask?" Dr. Lee said.

"I found it written on a note among my friend's things. She wanted to bring her boyfriend here, but they…they didn't make it."

"I'm sorry."

"It's okay."

"You're lucky, you know? If you'd arrived a few hours later, it would've been too late," Dr. Lee said.

Dylan frowned, focusing on the doctor's face. The woman was of Asian descent, both exotic and beautiful. "What do you mean, too late? I still had time left."

"Not quite. The cure needs to administered before the infected subject reaches the forty-eight hour mark. Otherwise, the damage to the brain is too severe, and the virus' control too advanced to reverse."

"You mean the psychotic episodes?" Dylan asked.

The doctor nodded. "Exactly. I've tried it on a few patients who were over the threshold. None of them survived."

Tara lifted her arm and stared at the fresh bandages that covered the bite wound. The black veins that used to mar her skin was gone, at least, and she wondered what the wound looked like. "How bad is it?"

"It isn't pretty. The surgeon had to cut away much of the necrotic tissue and skin. He did the best he could, but you'll carry the scar forever."

"I see."

"You will have full use of the arm, however," the doctor said in placating tones.

"That's okay. It's a small price to pay. I'm still alive, aren't I?" Dylan said.

Dr. Lee nodded. "Not only that, but you are also immune to the infection now."

"Immune?"

"Yes. You can't be reinfected. You're body has formed antibodies against the virus. You're one of only three people I know of who won't succumb to the zombie bite."

Dylan stared at her in wonder. "Just three?"

"Yes. I only recently perfected the formula. We had a lot of failed attempts before that. You're our third success story."

"You invented the cure?" Dylan asked, staring at Dr. Lee with admiration.

"Yes, I'm a virologist, and I've been studying the outbreak for months now. With the help of a couple of other scientists here at Fort Knox, I managed to formulate a cure. There were a lot of hiccups, though. Especially in the beginning."

"The others died?"

"Unfortunately. Someone leaked the story onto the Internet that there was a cure before it was ready yet, and a lot of people showed up looking for help. That must be how you're friend learned of it." Dr. Lee's expression was one of sorrow. "I wanted to save them all, but I couldn't."

Dylan felt a stab of sympathy for the scientist. She knew what guilt felt like. The weight of it on one's shoulders. "I'm sorry. I'm sure you did the best you could."

"It wasn't good enough," Dr. Lee said. "But thank you for saying so."

They stared at each other for a second, a strange feeling of fellowship growing between them. Dylan found it odd. She rarely connected with others, especially strangers. Yet, in the past few days she'd met not only Ethan, but Alex and Amy too. *It seems the apocalypse makes for strange bedfellows.*

Dr. Lee broke the silence first. "Well, I'm glad to see you're doing well. You should get some rest. You're friends will be allowed to visit you soon."

"Friends?"

"Yes, you came in with a young girl, and her brother?" Dr. Lee said.

"Oh, yes. They're okay? Alex was hurt," Dylan asked.

"They're just fine, both of them. The surgeon cleaned up the wound, and he's healing well. I'll tell them you're awake."

"Thanks."

Dr. Lee turned to leave when Dylan stopped her. "Dr. Lee."

"Yes?"

"Who is the other two?"

"Other two?"

"The other two who survived?"

"Oh. One is a little girl. She came in a week ago with her parents. They live here on the base in the civilian quarters. The other is my friend, Saul Dhlamini."

"I see. Thank you for saving my life, Doctor. I'll never forget it."

Dr. Lee smiled. "It was nothing Dylan."

"If there's ever anything I can do for you, let me know," Dylan said.

"I will. Thank you for the offer."

Dr. Lee ducked through the curtains, and Dylan was left by herself. After a few minutes, she dozed off, only to come awake with a start when Amy barged. The girl was a whirlwind of happy chatter and girlish squeals.

"Dylan, you're awake!"

"I am now," Dylan said with a groan, but she was secretly happy to see Amy.

"Wow, you look awesome. Much better than before. You're very pretty, you know, with the red hair and all."

"Who'd have thought."

"No need to be grumpy. I brought you something. Are you hungry?" Amy asked.

Dylan perked up. "I'm starving."

Amy frowned. "Starving as in normal hungry, or starving as

in you want to try and eat me again."

Dylan gaped at her. "I never tried to eat you."

"Yes, you did. Or my brother, at least. You did try to eat him."

Dylan fell back onto her cushions with a groan.

Alex arrived to save the day. "Come now, Amy. Don't tease Dylan like that. She's had a tough time."

"I was just joking with her," Amy said. "Here's your treat." She handed Dylan a polystyrene cup with a plastic spoon sticking out of mound of vanilla ice cream.

Dylan stared at the offering. "They've got ice cream here?"

"Yup, they've got everything here as long as you're willing to follow the rules and do your chores."

Not wasting a second, Dylan grabbed the cup and stuck a huge spoonful into her mouth. Her eyes fluttered shut, and she moaned. "Mm, that's delicious."

"Better than Alex you mean?" Amy asked with a wicked grin.

"Ugh, you little brat," Dylan cried, throwing a cushion at the giggling girl.

Alex rolled his eyes. "Kids. Seems I'm stuck with both of you."

Dylan snorted. "Speak for yourself."

"Oh, come. You know you like us," Amy said.

"Huh. Maybe just a little," Dylan relented, warmth spreading through her chest.

If this was the apocalypse, then maybe it wasn't so bad. It sure beat what she had before.

Amy stuck out her pinkie. "Friends?"

Dylan eyed the proffered hand, recognizing it for what it was. An offer of true friendship. She curled her pinkie around Amy's and shook on it.

"Friends."

The End.

Turn the page for a sneak peek at the next book in the series, now available on Amazon!

Do you want more?

So we've reached the end of Apocalypse Z - Book 1, and I really hope you enjoyed reading the book as much as I enjoyed writing it. If you did, please consider leaving a review as that makes it so much easier for an author like me to reach more readers like yourself and to keep writing. You can review the book here: https://www.amazon.com/dp/B07XKVD6NH

And, there's plenty more where this came from. Apocalypse Z - Book 2 is now available on Amazon, and I've included a preview for your enjoyment. Continue the adventure to find out what your favorite characters are up to next. Available here: https://www.amazon.com/dp/B07Y37MJZY

Apocalypse z - Book 2
Chapter 1 - Dylan

It was quiet inside the room.

Too quiet.

Dylan stared at the ceiling above her head, counting the minutes until morning. She couldn't sleep, despite the drugs that flowed through her veins. While under quarantine, the doctors took care to keep her calm and sedated. They were afraid of possible side-effects to the cure or even a relapse.

She didn't mind, at first. Not while her broken body knit

itself back together. But now, it was becoming a bore, and she still had two whole days to go. There was little to occupy herself with, and visiting hours were restricted to two thirty-minute windows per day. Besides Amy and Alex, the only other people who dared enter her room was Doctor Tara Lee and Doctor Knowles. Tara was nice enough. A bit formal, but at least she could hold a conversation. Dr. Knowles, however…now there was a man born with a stick up his ass.

She supposed it was a blessing that she had the place all to herself. No coughing, groaning, or snoring interrupted her sleep, and yet tonight, the silence felt threatening. Faint moonlight streamed through the blinds that covered the single window, casting the room in shades of silver and gray. But the light couldn't reach everywhere, and there in the corners lay the darkness.

She stared at one such a corner, her mouth dry with fear. The blackness pulsed and grew, reaching out with quivering tentacles to feed on her weakness. To her drug-soaked brain, it looked like a crouching beast ready to pounce on her shaking form.

"Oh, come on," Dylan muttered. She'd never been afraid of the dark. Ever.

With a determined grunt, she tossed aside her blankets and walked toward the small cubicle that formed a bathroom. It boasted a washbasin and toilet — nothing else.

After emptying her bladder, she washed her face and hands with soap. The cold water revived her senses, chasing away the fog caused by sleep and drugs. Dylan stared at her reflection in the mirror. She looked awful. Her hair desperately needed a wash, and deep shadows rimmed her eyes. During her trip and illness, she'd lost a lot of weight, and it wasn't pretty. Her bones jutted outward from her ribs and hips, while the fat had been chiseled from her cheeks until she resembled the Grim Reaper himself.

On a whim, she decided to take a shower. Grabbing a towel, soap, and toothbrush, she walked across the room and knocked on the door. "Nurse! Are you there?"

After a few seconds, the sharp clicking of heels on the tiled floor announced the arrival of the night nurse accompanied by a security guard. The lock clicked, and the door swung open to reveal a middle-aged head nurse with a dour expression. "Yes? Can I help you?"

"I'd like to take a shower, please," Dylan said.

The nurse frowned, and her disapproval was evident. "Can't it wait until morning?"

"I have physiotherapy in the morning," Dylan said. "Besides, it's after three already, and I could use a bath."

The nurse hesitated. "Fine, but don't use too much water. We are on strict rations."

"Yes, ma'am," Dylan replied in a dry tone of voice.

"And don't get that arm wet. The last thing we need is for it to get infected again," the nurse added. "George will keep watch outside and escort you back to your room when you're done."

Dylan shrugged. "As long as he doesn't spy on me, it's cool."

The nurse and security guard stared at her with distinct displeasure. "I'm certain he would never do such a thing."

"I'm not a pervert," George rumbled in a deep voice.

"Jeez, I'm just joking, okay?" Dylan said, rolling her eyes.

With a shake of her head, the nurse departed. George led the way to the communal bathroom equipped with baths and showers, and Dylan ducked inside. The room was empty, just the way she liked it. A soak in the tub was exactly what she needed to relax and forget about the creeping fear that wouldn't let go.

Inside an empty cubicle, Dylan undressed and placed her stuff on the small wooden bench provided. She opened the taps and waited for the basin to fill, adjusting the temperature until it was just right. Feet first, she stepped into the tub and eased back into the steaming water. Her eyes drifted shut, and a smile played on her lips. "This is the life."

After a few minutes, she sat upright to wash. It was difficult using only one hand, but she managed. Her fingers traced across the numerous injuries she'd accumulated on her journey to Fort Knox: The cut on her scalp thanks to crazy Maddie. That one still had stitches in it. Another one on her forehead and a jagged slash across her palm, both due to Frankie's zombie boyfriend. At least, they'd closed up, forming thin scars she'd carry for life. She was healing, but slowly, and had yet to regain her former vitality.

Her bitten arm, wrapped tightly in bandages, dangled over the side. She didn't have to see it to know what it looked like. Dr. Knowles had done the best he could, but the man was no plastic surgeon. It was a hack job, the damaged tissue brutally cut away, and the remnants stitched together until the arm looked like a Frankenstein special.

Dylan shuddered. It was a constant reminder of how close she'd come to death and insanity. A memory she'd much rather forget. Even now, Ray and his buddies haunted her dreams, their horrific deaths at her hands forever branded on her soul.

She shook her head. "Forget it. It's done."

Dylan quickly rinsed her hair, mindful of George at the door. If she took too long, he'd come looking for her. They were all scared of her. Scared and wary. At first, she couldn't understand why. She'd been cured, hadn't she? She wasn't going to become a zombie anymore.

Then Tara explained. Even though she'd been cured, there remained a chance that she could relapse. That the virus could overcome the cure. Hence her enforced quarantine. This, Dylan already knew.

But there was more.

Two others, besides Dylan, had successfully received the cure. Saul, Tara's companion and bodyguard, and a little girl. Both exhibited occasional side-effects that Tara was sure would present in Dylan as well. Fits of extreme aggression.

"And that's why they're all shit scared of me," Dylan said with a sharp frown. It felt strange to be the object of such intense fear and hatred. Nor did she look forward to going nuts again and ripping someone else's throat out. "Wouldn't that be awesome?"

Dylan dried off and slipped the hospital gown over her head. The nurses had taken all her clothing when she arrived, so she had no option but to wear the flimsy cotton dress and panties. Even worse, it was open at the back, the two flaps tied together with string. She was forever holding it shut with one hand, not willing to grant anyone a free look at her ass.

Not that there's much of it left anymore, she grumbled in her head. *And the hospital food isn't helping either. I wouldn't feed that slop to a dog.*

After brushing her teeth, she gathered up her stuff and prepared to leave when the lights went off. Plunged into darkness, Dylan froze on the spot. Her former fears came rushing back, and her heart rate sped up until it raced in her chest. Licking her dry lips, she called out, "George? What's happening?"

No answer.

"George?"

Dylan edged forward, one hand stretched out into the unknown until she encountered the wall. She pressed her back against it and shut her eyes in an attempt to calm down. In the distance, a siren began to wail. It grew louder and louder until the sound vibrated through the walls and floor beneath her naked feet. It could only mean one thing.

A breach.

"No. It can't be. Not here. It's supposed to be safe here," Dylan whispered, her voice harsh in her ears. Terror flooded her veins. She'd been warned about the siren. It meant that the infected had breached the compound. They were inside.

She crept sideways on trembling legs, arms stretched out until she felt the door beneath her fingertips. Her hand gripped the handle, and she cracked it open an inch. Inky darkness met her eyes. "George?"

Still no answer.

Her anxiety ratcheted up several knots.

Where could he be?

"George!"

Still nothing but the echo of her voice up and down the passage. The hair on the back of her head rose, and goosebumps pebbled her skin.

Then the back-up generators kicked in, and the lights in the hallway flickered on, much to her relief. She looked to either side. The place was deserted with no signs of George or the nurse. Where were they? What was happening?

The siren continued its wailing cry, and Dylan knew she was in trouble. They all were. "Shit, what now? I've got no clothes, no weapons. And what about Alex and Amy?"

Thinking about her friends calmed her galloping heart, and she was able to focus on the situation at hand. Her brain switched into survival mode, and she remembered something she'd seen a few days ago.

On silent feet, she jogged to the spot until she reached it. Bolted to the wall was a red box with an ax inside. One of those "Break Glass in Case of Emergency" boxes. Ditching the soap and toothpaste, she wrapped the towel around her fist and smashed the glass with one solid blow. After clearing away any sharp bits, she plucked out the ax, hefting it with both hands. It wasn't a gun, but it was better than nothing.

Faint cries emitted from the occupied ward across the hall as other patients woke up from the noise. The door opened, and an older woman stuck her head through the opening. "What's going on?"

Dylan shrugged. "I'm not sure, Ma'am, but you'd better go inside and barricade the door from the inside."

"Is it an attack?" the woman asked.

"I think so, ma'am, but I'm sure the soldiers will sort it out. In the meantime, stay inside and block the doors," Dylan said with more confidence than she felt. "I'll go have a look outside and find out what's happening."

The woman eyed the ax in Dylan's hands and nodded. "Alright, but be careful."

"I will, ma'am. Thanks."

The woman disappeared back into the ward, and the noise of dragging furniture sounded soon after. At least, they were following her instructions, and it should keep them safe for the time being.

Dylan turned away and looked down the hall. Going back

to her room served no purpose. There was nothing there that she could use. No clothes. No weapons. Nothing. Nor did she feel like cowering behind its door, waiting for the inevitable. That left the nursing station. "There's got to be someone there. Or something I can use, at least."

With slow steps, Dylan walked down the hall with the ax held ready to strike. The lights dipped in and out, alternating between utter darkness and a feeble glow. Her pulse quickened as her brain imagined terrifying horrors lurking around every corner. Her tongue darted out to touch her dry lips, and goosebumps pebbled her arms.

Finally, she reached the end of the passage. A set of double doors were propped wide open and led to a small waiting room. She peered into the murky space beyond the opening. Chairs lined the walls, and a coffee table sported a couple of dog-eared magazines. Her destination, the nursing station, lay to the far left. It was a simple counter bolted to the wall and topped with computer monitors.

Dylan narrowed her gaze, studying the space with minute attention. Not a single person was in sight, and nothing seemed out of place, but instinct warned her that she wasn't alone. Gripping the ax tightly, she walked toward the station, placing each foot with care. Thick carpet replaced the cold tiles, muffling her footsteps. As she drew closer, low grunts and snuffling met her ears. It sounded like a pig feeding at a trough.

With supreme reluctance, Dylan edged around the corner of the counter. Her foot landed in a thick puddle of fluid, and she froze. Her eyes darted down, and bile rose up her throat as the lights flickered on again.

Blood.

She was standing in a pool of blood.

She lifted her gaze, and they fixed on the crooked figure of a man hunched over the lifeless body of George. The former guard stared at her, mute in death, while the zombie tugged at his guts with curved fingers. Beyond them lay the head nurse, her uniform no longer white but crimson. Her throat gaped open, the bones of her spine shining through the tendrils of torn flesh and sinew.

Dylan stared at the tableau of horror for several seconds, not daring to breathe. The zombie was right in front of her, so close she could reach out and touch him. With infinite care, she lifted the ax above her head. At the last second, the soaked carpet beneath her foot squelched when her weight shifted.

The infected man whirled around and snarled. As quick as a striking snake, he leaped. Before she could blink, he was on her, and they tumbled to the ground in a whirl of arms and legs.

Dylan hit the ground hard, and the air left her lungs in a pained exhalation. She held onto the ax with both hands, desperate to keep the zombie at bay. He wriggled on top of her, his teeth snapping at her face, and his fingers clutched at her shoulders.

Twisting to the side, she kneed him in the ribs, dislodging him for a brief second. As he lost his grip, she smashed the ax into his mouth. A couple of teeth broke from the impact, sending the infected into a frenzy of vicious snarls. Blood and spit sprayed across her face, but she couldn't back down.

With the ax head clamped between his jaws, she wrestled the zombie to the side and got one foot underneath her. She ducked when he swung at her head, and his fist narrowly missed her temple. Another hit landed on her shoulder, and she grunted from the force of the blow. Her arm went numb but dared not let up for even a millisecond.

Dylan pulled back her weapon and struck again, using all of her strength. The zombie fell backward, his mouth a gaping hole filled with shattered fangs. The moment she was free, she brought the ax down on his head. At the same time, he lunged upward. The blade sunk into his forehead with a dull thunk, and his eyes rolled back in their sockets. For a single, breathless moment, they were suspended in the act of death. Then the ax slid free, and the infected collapsed to the floor, still at last.

Dylan scrambled to her feet, breathing hard. The fight had taken its toll, and her limbs quivered with exhaustion. She choked back a sob of relief. "Holy shit, I did it. I'm still alive."

But movement caught the edge of her vision, and she turned, her heart jumping in her throat. Next to the counter stood George. His eyes were as black as night, and his hands curled into fists the size of dinner plates. Behind him, the head nurse was getting to her feet, her head swaying back and forth on her ravaged neck. Both honed in on her fragile form with predatory instinct. Their lips peeled back, and they roared with insane hunger.

In that instant, Dylan knew she was as good as dead. Rage took the place of fear. If she was going to die, she might as well go down fighting. She raised the ax and screamed with defiance. "Come on, you fucking zombies! Show me what you've got!"

End of preview: Available here: https://www.amazon.com/dp/B07Y37MJZY

Your FREE Ebook is waiting!

If you'd like to learn more about my books, upcoming projects, new releases, cover reveals, and promotions, simply join my mailing list. Plus, you'll get an exclusive ebook absolutely FREE just for subscribing!

Yes, please. Sign me up!
  https://www.subscribepage.com/i0d7r8

Author Bio

About the author

Baileigh Higgins, author of the bestselling Zombie Apocalypse Series, Dangerous Days, lives in the Free State, South Africa, with hubby and best friend Brendan and loves nothing more than lazing on the couch with pizza and a bad horror movie. Her unhealthy obsession with the end of the world has led to numerous books on the subject and a secret bunker only she knows the location of.

Visit her website at www.baileighhiggins.com to get the latest news on all her projects including an exclusive FREE ebook for new subscribers.

WEBSITE - **www.baileighhiggins.com**

CPSIA information can be obtained
at www.ICGtesting.com
Printed in the USA
BVHW032253030420
576871BV00001B/63